Psalm 37:4

In Loving Memory of the following people who have inspired and/or assisted in bringing my poetry to book form and have gone on to that big ranch in the sky.

Becky Gasaway
Byron Gasaway
Francine Ross
Jay Spruill
Millie Parker
Samuel Gasaway
Sylvia W. Turner
Teresa Staten

Michael's books are a collection of inspirational stories about life and love written in a unique rhyme format. They cover the gamut of life experiences, written from both a female and male perspective depending on the story. The stories take place from the modern day to the 1800s. These pages will take the reader through the many stages of life including love, desire, dreams, choices, adversity, trials, faith, fear, happiness, destiny, passion, purpose, trust, and loss to name a few. Each reader comes away with a distinctive viewpoint as to what the story was about; depending on their unique life experiences. Various times the same reader will interpret the story differently upon reading it a second or third time depending on their stage in life or emotional bearing they are experiencing at that time. Two different readers have actually tried to tell the other that they must be reading a different story as their viewpoints and understanding of the story are so different. Michael's books are not merely books of poetry per se but rather a unique way of storytelling in a rhythm format that is easy to read, comprehend and remember. Each story is accompanied with appropriate Bible verses that give even more strength and understanding to each story. The author's background as a Cowboy Christian gentleman from Texas adds a distinctive western flavor to many of his stories. Many times the tales will transport the reader to another time and place altogether. Michael' has a following in all fifty states and over thirty countries worldwide.

Praise for
Desires of Your Heart, Angels & Cowboys and Life's Highway and Dusty Trails

"Michael has a gift and writes from his heart. He is a true man of God and his words have touched many lives. He sees the beauty in others and shares his life experiences, insights and feelings with honesty and love."- Nancy from Illinois

"……his poems have touched my heart……..the poems this gifted man writes are a true inspiration to us all. Michael brings our Heavenly Father's guidance and words of scripture in layman's terms." - Melody from Texas

"A good honest read from the heart. I could never relate much to the Bible until I started reading this man's books. The way he ties in scripture verses to every story seems to now make the Bible come alive for me as it never did before." - Jack from Missouri

"Your poems saved me Michael; they touched my heart and gave me Peace, the kind that surpasses all understanding. And then you would arm me with the written word and those scriptures became my armor and my shield and soon, I wasn't so sad or discouraged or even ashamed. I'm proud to be a child of God, a horse lover, a cowgirl with those old fashioned morals."- Maura from Arizona

"Desires of Your Heart will help you open your heart to hear God speak to you day by day. Your spirit will overflow, as you are embraced by the One who loves you more than you can imagine."- Debra from Kansas

"One of the most well written books I have ever read. Each story touches a part of my life in some way. A GREAT spiritual book that I think will even be a BIGGER success than it already is as the public discovers this one. Keep writing Michael Gasaway you have a WINNER on your hands." – Maddie from Georgia

"Inspiring, uplifting. Love it!" – Margaret from Iowa

"It's like he has a backseat to my life and knows what I'm feeling." – Jackie from Florida

"I love Michael Gasaway's poetry! His stories are of life and the way he turns life situations into words is so touching and truly

Amazing. I recommend this book to anyone who loves a good read." – Nancy from Colorado

"Your book has brought much comfort to my heart..." - Maria from Nevada

"You will not be disappointed in his heartfelt writes! A wonderful book! Buy more than one and share to bless others!" – Cherie from Iowa

"I really enjoyed reading this book of poems and the scriptures that apply to the poem. It is very inspirational and thought provoking. I highly recommend it to everyone seeking comfort and inspiration for your life." - Linda from Texas

"I really like it. Makes me leave the days problems and go away. I would like to buy more of his work." - Donna from Oklahoma

"This book is more than just any average book it will speak directly to your heart and the places that need to be filled with encouragement and hope. This book besides my Bible itself is so encouraging and full of hope. I truly know it will bless your heart and encourage you!! Truly has a gift for writing from the heart and touches the soul!! Highly recommend this book, it will bless you!! Thank you Michael for your amazing gift of encouragement and writing!!" – Tiffany from Minnesota

"Your words are a blessing. God has given you the gift of writing poems. Thank you for this.....it spoke to my heart." – Judy from California

"He just seems to reach in and touch my heart with his words." – Cindy from Oregon

"Truly a gifted writer that just seems to know what a woman is feeling and thinking. His stories really touch home with so much of my past and hopefully my future." – Irene from Oklahoma

"His books read like a good country song. They seem to touch on all aspects of life from a western (my) perspective." – Jim from Texas

Heart's Desire
And
Passions Fire

Stories of Love and Life Written in Rhyme

MICHAEL GASAWAY

© 2019 Michael Gasaway

All rights reserved. No portion of this book may be reproduced, stored in a retrieval system, or transmitted in any form or by any means—electronic, mechanical, photocopy, recording, or any other---except for brief quotation in printed reviews, without prior written permission of the author or publisher.

Published by Diamond G Publishing.

Scriptures were taken from the King James Version of the Holy Bible. Public Domain.

Scriptures were taken from the Holy Bible, New International Version ®, NIV ®. Copyright © 1973, 1978, 1984, 2011, by Biblica, Inc. ™ Used by permission of Zondervan, All rights reserved worldwide. www.zondervan.com The "NIV" and "New International Version" are trademarks registered in the United States Patent Trademark Office by Biblica, Inc. ™ Used by permission

Scriptures taken from the New King James Version®.
Copyright © 1982 by Thomas Nelson, Used by permission.
. All rights reserved.

Scripture quotations are from the ESV® Bible (The Holy Bible, English Standard Version®), copyright © 2001 by Crossway, a publishing ministry of Good News Publishers. Used by permission. All rights reserved.

Cover art work by Jennifer Givner. Contact Jennifer at her web site for more information on this or other art. **www.acapellabookcoverdesign.com**

Graphic design, front and back cover art by Jennifer Givner.

Back cover photograph by Carol McEver Maceikis

ISBN- 9781796392999

Printed in USA

The stories in rhyme within this book are a work of fiction. Characters, places and incidents either are products of the author's imagination or are used fictitiously. Any resemblance to actual events or locals or persons, living or dead, is entirely coincidence.

This book is dedicated to my family, friends, and anyone that has journeyed down Life's Highway or Dusty Trail in search of their "Hearts Desire and Passions Fire". To my sons of whom I'm so proud of the men and the great examples you continue to be and display each and every day. To my youngest son Sammy that continues to inspire all of us from heaven above. "You inspire me every day Sammy and I think it's really time for me to go climb our mountain again. See you at the top!"

I hope these poems put a smile on your face, a song in your heart or maybe a tear in your eye when you remember back to that first hello or last goodbye. Remember you're never too young or too old to seek out and follow your dreams. God Bless, Never Give Up and Keep Dreamin'.

Thank you to my many Facebook friends who have taken this journey in rhyme with me over the years. Your comments have been very motivational and kept me writing when I was wondering if it was doing any good at all.

Follow me on Facebook at:
https://www.facebook.com/michaelthepoetryman and at my website:
http://www.michaelgasaway.com/

Thank you everyone that has offered suggestions for poems. I hope you see a story written in rhyme within these pages that brings you inspiration, hope, faith and peace.

A special thank you goes out to those very exceptional people who inspired many of these poems. May God grant you the desires of your heart and make all your dreams come true.

I would like to extend a very special thank you to Denny Karchner for his time and efforts in producing the graphic art work and cover painting for my previous books.

Thank you God for guiding my pen that wrote these words. Thank you God for providing me with the inspiration that has reached so many hearts and keeps touching and changing so many lives.

Guide to Story Themes

Adversity: 19, 25, 27, 53, 55, 75, 79, 87, 103, 111, 113, 119, 123, 127, 129, 131, 133, 143

Attitude: 25, 27, 29, 31, 33, 41, 45, 47, 51, 59, 61, 69, 73, 83, 85, 87, 93, 97, 101, 103, 123, 127, 137, 139, 153

Believe: 15, 27, 29, 31, 41, 47, 49, 51, 53, 57, 59, 61, 63, 65, 69, 71, 77, 79, 83, 97, 101, 121, 125, 127, 139, 141, 147, 151, 157, 159

Brokenness: 25, 33, 39, 41, 53, 57, 75, 79, 87, 103, 111, 113, 117, 129, 131, 133, 143, 145, 147

Change: 29, 37, 39, 41, 55, 59, 61, 77, 83, 85, 87, 89, 91, 93, 97, 103, 113, 117, 133, 147

Choices: 17, 21, 27, 31, 39, 45, 47, 49, 51, 55, 57, 59, 67, 73, 75, 77, 79, 83, 89, 91, 101, 103, 113, 123, 125, 129, 133, 139, 141, 157

Closure & Fear: 9, 45, 105, 117, 129, 133

Desires: 29, 39, 41, 51, 63, 65, 67, 71, 73, 77, 79, 83, 97, 107, 141, 159

Dreams: 29, 43, 49, 51, 53, 61, 63, 65, 67, 69, 71, 73, 77, 79, 83, 91, 97, 135, 141, 145, 147, 153, 155, 157, 159

Destiny: 23, 25, 41, 43, 49, 51, 55, 61, 63, 65, 67, 77, 79, 83, 91, 95, 97, 105, 109, 123, 133, 135, 141, 151

Faith: 17, 19, 29, 41, 55, 65, 75, 77, 79, 83, 95, 97, 103, 113, 115, 119, 121, 123, 125, 127, 131, 133, 137, 141, 143, 153

Happiness & Blessings: 15, 41, 43, 45, 51, 107, 123, 131, 149, 159

Hope & Peace: 27, 77, 79, 83, 85, 107, 131, 127, 151

Loss & Pain: 11, 17, 33, 35, 45, 53, 75, 103, 105, 111, 115, 117, 119, 129, 131, 143, 145, 151

Love: 9, 11, 13, 15, 17, 21, 23, 31, 33, 35, 41, 43, 45, 51, 53, 63, 65, 67, 71, 75, 77, 81, 83, 89, 94, 95, 97, 105, 107, 109, 121, 123, 125, 131, 135, 137, 141, 147, 149, 151, 155, 157, 159

Stress: 17, 19, 103, 121, 143

Memories: 11, 17, 33, 35, 39, 45, 53, 61, 67, 71, 73, 81, 83, 85, 87, 89, 91, 99, 109, 113, 123, 135, 141

Music & Dance: 13, 21, 31, 67, 81, 109, 149, 155, 157

New Beginnings: 11, 15, 27, 29, 35, 37, 41, 43, 45, 47, 49, 51, 55, 63, 65, 71, 75, 81, 83, 87, 89, 91, 93, 97, 99, 101, 103, 105, 117, 121, 125, 127, 133, 141, 143, 145, 147, 149

Never Give Up: 9, 11, 21, 25, 27, 29, 35, 41, 49, 73, 75, 83, 87, 91, 93, 97, 101, 103, 105, 115, 119, 123, 127, 131, 143, 147, 153

Passion: 9, 15, 23, 35, 41, 43, 63, 67, 714, 77, 81, 89, 91, 99, 105, 109, 123, 127, 135, 141, 151

Thankfulness: 15, 45, 55, 61, 63, 93, 97, 123

Trust: 19, 21, 25, 29, 39, 43, 47, 49, 55, 57, 69, 83, 93, 95, 99, 103, 117, 119, 121, 125, 127, 133, 135 137

Table of Contents in Alphabetical Order

A New Breath 39
A New Dream to Chase 27
A Real Cowboys Job 19
A Silent Prayer 33
All American Girl 51
Along Life's Dusty Trail 65
Always Keep Trying 75
Amazing Grace 97
Analogy of Love 107
Bands of Gold 127
Begin Again 143
Beneath a Texas Blue Moon 71
Brand New Boots 11
Brand New Day 79
Chance Meeting 89
Changed His Direction 103
Christmas Dream 155
Chronis Pain 111
Cinch Up, Never Give Up 131
Clean Slate 145
Crossroads 123
Dance of Love 13
Dreams Along Life's Highway 73
Eyes to See 47
Face it Until You Make It 29
Final 8 Second Ride 69
First Date...or...Life's Fate 77
Go Chase Your Dreams 49
God Knows Why! 93
Heart and Mind Aligned 95
Heart's Desire and Passions Fire 9
Heaven 125
Her Cowgirl Ways 45
Her Independence Day 133
Her Mustang Ways 139
Her Sweet Sweet Love 135
Hopes and Dreams 151
How to Love a Woman 31

It's Never Easy 147
Last First Date 35
Last Love 43
Lasting Memory 109
Life's Ride 113
Like a Spring Rain 119
Loves Grand Prize 67
Loves Trance 21
Make That List 37
Memories of an Angel 53
Memory Slaves 57
Missing Texas Blues 61
My Happy Place 83
Never Give Up on Love 91
Never Really Lose 101
Piercing Heartaches Dark Veil 41
Rainbows of Love 15
Ready to Begin 55
Romantic Dream 63
Set an Example 59
She Remembered 99
Some Cowgirls 87
Sparkle of Delight 81
Stillness of Night 117
Stories and Lies 129
Talk and Listen to God 137
Texas Cowboy and a Tennessee Lady 141
Texas Dance Hall 149
Texas Spring Day 17
The Broken Spoke 157
The Cowboy and the Irish Lass 23
The Real Deal 159
This Life We Call The Ride 121
Time to Cowboy Up 85
Trials and Hardships 25
Turquoise and Gold 105
Unanswered Questions 115
Win Lose or Draw 153

Heart's Desire and Passions Fire

Long blond hair with emerald green eyes sparkling in the sunlight from above;
That little girl within her wanted to really experience an everlasting unconditional kind of true love.

Fear and pain had locked her away behind the walls she had built beyond her own heart's closed door;
Somehow he had reached deep within her spirit and shown her the beauty of a distant shore.

Now with a promising smile illuminating her beautiful and delicate face;
She was now beginning to really release her anguish and start to feel God's amazing grace.

Slowly she began to open up like a delicate yellow rose and bit by bit put the hurtful past to rest;
Deep inside something told her that now was the time for her, and this was going to be for the best.

The future she now sees was brighter than anything she had ever imagined or could have dreamed;
Yes, she thought in the recesses of her mind, God surely does answer prayers it seems.

As a true cowboy angel had opened loves door and made her really believe;
Now side by side they ride life's trail together and to each other's heart, they will always cleave.

So never stop dreaming or praying those prayers for your solitary heart's desire;
One day you'll realize that the time has come as together you ignite passions fire.

Then into tomorrow's dawn, you'll ride together into a fresh new life, love and, your own promise land;
Never give up on your hopes and dreams and always cling onto each other's heart and hand.

~~~

*Love is patient and kind; love does not envy or boast; it is not arrogant or rude. It does not insist on its own way; it is not irritable or resentful; it does not rejoice at wrongdoing, but rejoices with the truth. Love bears all things, believes all things, hopes all things, endures all things. Love never ends.
1 Corinthians 13:4-8*

For I reckon that the sufferings of this present time are not worthy to be compared with the glory which shall be revealed in us. Romans 8:18

*Fear thou not; for I am with thee: be not dismayed; for I am thy God: I will strengthen thee; yea, I will help thee; yea, I will uphold thee with the right hand of my righteousness.
Isaiah 41:10*

Peace I leave with you, my peace I give unto you: not as the world giveth, give I unto you. Let not your heart be troubled, neither let it be afraid. John 14:27

There is no fear in love; but perfect love casteth out fear: because fear hath torment. He that feareth is not made perfect in love. 1 John 4:18

*May he grant you your heart's desire and fulfill all your plans!
Psalm 20:4*

*Casting all your anxieties on him, because he cares for you.
1 Peter 5:7 ESV*

For God hath not given us the spirit of fear; but of power, and of love, and of a sound mind. 2 Timothy 1:7

Delight thyself also in the Lord: and he shall give thee the desires of thine heart. Psalm 37:4

And let us not grow weary of doing good, for in due season we will reap, if we do not give up. Galatians 6:9

And above all these put on love, which binds everything together in perfect harmony. Colossians 3:14

My beloved is mine, and I am his: Song of Solomon 2:16

Brand New Boots

Tears gradually pooled in her sparkling brown eyes as her thoughts drifted back to the past few weeks;
Then those tears slowly rolled down her already tear stained cheeks.

Memories can be like ocean waves as they come rolling on to the shore;
Some come gently washing in as others come rushing in with a great roar.

Another sleepless night and soon a new day would begin with the light of an early dawn;
She knew it was time to start picking up the pieces and just move forward and carry on.

It was now or never to really start living the life she had once planned;
Time to cowgirl up and onto her brand new boots she knew that she was going to land.

Putting the past away behind those doors she knew were now forever closed;
Striking out on one of those many new trails that before her now rose.

Into a bright new future she was sure that God would lead her into a fateful place and time;
Where on a not too distant star-filled night the planets and Gods promises would truly align.

Time to really just let God be her guide and lead her down the right trail;
With His guidance, she knew that this time she would find the answers and that mountain she'd scale.

Slowly the sun rose and lit up the sky on this the beginning of her new life;
Behind her now was her past with all the pain, hurt feelings and strife.

Not long after those painful tears stained her rose petal cheeks
on that fateful night;
Into her world, a real Cowboy Christian man came into her life
and made everything feel alright.

So never give up on love and life and the desires of your heart
deep inside;
Just keep trusting in God and always believe that all your needs
He will provide.

∼∼∼

I am weary with my groaning; all the night make I my bed to swim; I water my couch with my tears. Psalm 6:6

It is vain for you to rise up early, to sit up late, to eat the bread of sorrows: for so he gives his beloved sleep. Psalm 127:2

*Be careful for nothing; but in everything by prayer and supplication with thanksgiving let your requests be made known unto God. And the peace of God, which passes all understanding, shall keep your hearts and minds through Christ Jesus.
Philippians 4:6-7*

*And ye shall know the truth, and the truth shall make you free.
John 8:32*

*For I know the thoughts that I think toward you, saith the Lord, thoughts of peace, and not of evil, to give you an expected end.
Jeremiah 29:11*

*There hath no temptation taken you but such as is common to man: but God is faithful, who will not suffer you to be tempted above that ye are able; but will with the temptation also make a way to escape, that ye may be able to bear it.
1 Corinthians 10:13*

Trust in the Lord with all thine heart; and lean not unto thine own understanding. In all thy ways acknowledge him, and he shall direct thy paths. Proverbs 3:5-6

Now faith is the substance of things hoped for, the evidence of things not seen. Hebrews 11:1
Delight thyself also in the Lord: and he shall give thee the desires of thine heart. Psalm 37:4

Dance of Love

They had equally faced losses in both love and life it seems;
But neither had really given up on love or those deep-seated romantic dreams.

Then on one summer eve, it all came together for each to find as love was in the air;
Yes, they had found a real true love to share, her with dancing eyes and flaming crimson hair.

He was wearing a Stetson, starched Wranglers and pearl snaps with penetrating brown eyes;
They came together touching each other's heart setting each other free to truly fly.

She never really thought that true love would ever find her again on those wide Oklahoma plains;
But there they were in each other's arms just dancing in the gently falling rain.

A true dance of love and romance that brought them closer as they danced on;
It was starting to make her feel a little giddy like her first drink of champagne once upon.

On went their dance of love year after year, on through the pouring rain, drought or blazing sun;
They held each other's heart and hand putting their faith and trust in the Holy Ghost, Father, and Son.

Now here they were realizing a dream of love so very rare and true;
So if you never give up on life and love, it may also happen to you.

Keep trusting in God and each day ride the trail and the right way to you He will show;
Your true love may be just beyond the horizon waiting for you to discover your destiny and on you go.

∼∼∼

And God shall wipe away all tears from their eyes; and there shall be no more death, neither sorrow, nor crying, neither shall there be any more pain: for the former things are passed away. Revelation 21:4

Humble yourselves therefore under the mighty hand of God, that he may exalt you in due time: Casting all your care upon him; for he cares for you. 1 Peter 5:6-7

But as it is written, Eye hath not seen, nor ear heard, neither have entered into the heart of man, the things which God hath prepared for them that love him. 1 Corinthians 2:9

Love is patient and kind; love does not envy or boast; it is not arrogant or rude. It does not insist on its own way; it is not irritable or resentful; it does not rejoice at wrongdoing, but rejoices with the truth. 1 Corinthians 13:4-6

Delight thyself also in the Lord: and he shall give thee the desires of thine heart. Psalm 37:4

For every one that asked received; and he that sought found it; and to him that knocked it shall be opened. Matthew 7:8

There is no fear in love; but perfect love cast out fear: because fear hath torment. He that fears is not made perfect in love. 1 John 4:18

He who finds a wife finds a good thing and obtains favor from the Lord. Proverbs 18:22

An excellent wife who can find? She is far more precious than jewels. Proverbs 31:10

Trust in the Lord with all thine heart; and lean not unto thine own understanding. Proverbs 3:5

Now faith is the substance of things hoped for, the evidence of things not seen. Hebrews 11:1

Rainbows of Love

She had just arrived and they were going to be together once again;
Down they'd go to South Padre Island for a few days to spend.

Oh, she was so very happy that was so plain to see as she stepped from the plane;
All that seemed to matter to either of them was the love they shared that neither could explain.

He had planned for them an especially romantic and extraordinary time;
It seems these days that pleasing her was all he had on his mind.

Neither could explain the feelings and how they could both be this much in love;
They just equally felt they were being blessed by God from up above.

Both had silently been praying for a sign showing this was really meant to be;
Then out on the Gulf of Mexico there two beautiful full multicolored rainbows they did see.

Amazed at what she saw she said: "One for each of us across the water so blue".;
To her it was was just another sign blessing them and saying' God loves you.

With two rainbows together arching high in the sky above;
It was no wonder that at that moment they fell even more in love.

A rainbow alone is so nice but two at that moment was such a special sight;
Looking deep into each other's eyes they both realized and knew this was oh so right.

They looked up and both thanked God for this sign coming down from heaven like a dove;
Then she looked into his eyes and said, "thank you God for sending him for me to love".

Along the beach later they walked hand 'n hand making hearts in the sand;
Later he carried her from the waters edge and brushed the sand from her feet with his hand.

Inside she told him to sit and relax for a bit and back she would soon be;
Before long she appeared with a bowl of warm water and then washed his feet so lovenly.

Drying his feet with her long dark hair she kissed him passionately so;
Then she pulled him up and through love's door they did go.

∾∾∾

And now these three remain: faith, hope and love. But the greatest of these is love. 1 Corinthians 13:13

Above all, love each other deeply, because love covers over a multitude of sins. 1 Peter 4:8

With all lowliness and meekness, with longsuffering, forbearing one another in love; Ephesians 4:2

Let him kiss me with the kisses of his mouth: for thy love is better than wine.   You are altogether beautiful, my love; there is no flaw in you. Song of Solomon 1:2 & 4:7

My beloved is mine, and I am his: Song of Solomon 2:16

I do set my bow in the cloud, and it shall be for a token of a covenant between me and the earth. Genesis 9:13

If ye know these things, happy are ye if ye do them. John 13:17

And he turned to the woman, and said unto Simon, See that woman? I entered into thine house, thou gavest me no water for my feet: but she hath washed my feet with tears, and wiped them with the hairs of her head. Luke 7:44

And over all these virtues put on love, which binds them all together in perfect unity. Colossians 3:14

She is more precious than jewels, and nothing you desire can compare with her. Proverbs 3:15

Texas Spring Day

Sitting upon his horse he remembered back to that special Texas spring day;
Bluebonnets and Indian paintbrushes were blooming as he listened to her sing away.

She had come into his life when he was so down and almost out of control;
Back to a life full of love and beauty she once again had made him feel whole.

Her voice was like that of a special angel singing down into his very soul;
Remembering back to that fall day long ago when he had to let her go.

Sometimes life seems to be full of twist and turns taking you places you never thought or schemed;
We never know what over the next hill will come and if it'll be the answer to our hopes and dreams.

The years have passed on but in his heart, he always feels her so very near;
It's always in the spring when it seems that he hears her singing sweetly in his ear.

He knows it won't be long 'til he joins her up in heaven above;
She'll be waiting beneath that heavenly oak once again for them to share their love.

There she is on that bench beneath that legendary oak tree, rising to meet him as he enters those heavenly scenes;
She's even more beautiful it seems as together they'll walk among the bluebonnets in a forever, heavenly spring.

∼∼∼

O come, let us sing unto the Lord: let us make a joyful noise to the rock of our salvation. Psalm 95:1

Is any among you afflicted? let him pray. Is any merry? let him sing psalms. James 5:13

You are altogether beautiful, my love; there is no flaw in you. Song of Solomon 4:7

He has made everything beautiful in its time. Also, he has put eternity into man's heart Ecclesiastes 3:11

Love is patient and kind; love does not envy or boast; it is not arrogant or rude. It does not insist on its own way; it is not irritable or resentful; it does not rejoice at wrongdoing, but rejoices with the truth. Love bears all things, believes all things, hopes all things, endures all things. Love never ends. As for prophecies, they will pass away; as for tongues, they will cease; as for knowledge, it will pass away. 1 Corinthians 13:4-8

And above all these put on love, which binds everything together in perfect harmony. Colossians 3:14

But as it is written, Eye hath not seen, nor ear heard, neither have entered into the heart of man, the things which God hath prepared for them that love him. 1 Corinthians 2:9

And God shall wipe away all tears from their eyes; and there shall be no more death, neither sorrow, nor crying, neither shall there be any more pain: for the former things are passed away. Revelation 21:4

A Real Cowboy's Job

It seemed like it had been raining for days and he was soaked thru and thru;
But he had no choice as he had a real cowboy's job to do.

Not some motion picture of what some make believe cowboy had to do each day;
But real life chores like, things to fix, fences to mend, mucking stalls and bailing hay.

With no real days off or some vacation relaxing in the summer sun;
There were horses and cattle to feed and around a ranch always something to get done.

Sometimes he wondered if God had a sense of humor looking down from up on high;
He had prayed and prayed so hard for rain and for this drought to subside.

Now it seemed there was no end in sight to all this new found rain and additional strain;
Often he would think about what was worse, the drought or too much rain.

Such is a cowboy's life and seems not much has changed in over a hundred years;
At times he still finds his beloved wife late into the night crying those worrisome tears.

But his faith in God and knowing that somehow all things work out for the best in the end;
Often he wondered how folks could make it without having God as your trusted friend.

Feeling that this was really God's ranch as he watched each sunrise when his day had begun;
He was just Gods caretaker until Jesus came to tell him Good Ride Cowboy, you're done.

~~~

Who covered the heaven with clouds, who prepared rain for the earth, who makes grass to grow upon the mountains. Psalm 147:8

Whatsoever thy hand findeth to do, do it with thy might; for there is no work, nor device, nor knowledge, nor wisdom, in the grave, Ecclesiastes 9:10

And whatsoever ye do, do it heartily, as to the Lord, and not unto men; Colossians 3:23

For I know the plans I have for you, declares the Lord, plans for welfare and not for evil, to give you a future and a hope. Jeremiah 29:11

I can do all things through Christ which strengthened me. Philippians 4:13

Do all things without murmurings and disputing: Philippians 2:14

Rejoice in hope, be patient in tribulation, be constant in prayer. Romans 12:12

Seek the Lord and his strength, seek his face continually. 1 Chronicles 16:11

They that sow in tears shall reap in joy. Psalm 126:5

Two are better than one; because they have a good reward for their labor. For if they fall, the one will lift up his fellow: but woe to him that is alone when he falleth; for he hath not another to help him up. Ecclesiastes 4:9-10

The land shall not be sold for ever: for the land is mine, for ye are strangers and sojourners with me Leviticus 25:23-24

Loves Trance

Seemingly they just danced, twirled and did glide across the hardwood sawdust covered floor;
In her mind she was thinking how she loved her life and how could she ever ask for more.

Then as if on cue the music stopped and on them, the spotlight came shining through by design;
Dropping to one knee her cowboy softly said,"Darlin' forever will you be mine?"

He held out the ring and with a big Texas smile she said yes;
Putting it on her finger he felt like he'd just passed loves final true test.

Then the band started playing their favorite song as everyone clapped and cheered;
In both of their hearts, they realized that this was going to be their banner year.

With their boots hardly even touching the floor as on they danced and twirled all about;
It was like they were now lost forever somewhere in loves trance neither with any doubt.

Their life was now just beginning and the best was still yet to be;
They were going to begin a new life together with a fall wedding and then a happy family.

So never give up on true love or that your life can't get any better than it seems;
Just keep trusting in God and maybe one day soon a cowboy will come dancing into your dreams.

∾∾∾

…….and a time to dance; Ecclesiastes 3:4

An excellent wife who can find? She is far more precious than jewels. Proverbs 31:10

You are altogether beautiful, my love; there is no flaw in you. Song of Solomon 4:7

Let marriage be held in honor among all, Hebrews 13:4

A virtuous woman is a crown to her husband: Proverbs 12:4

Behold, you are beautiful, my love, behold, you are beautiful! Song of Solomon 4:1

And let us not grow weary of doing good, for in due season we will reap, if we do not give up. Galatians 6:9

Trust in the LORD with all thine heart; and lean not unto thine own understanding. Proverbs 3:5

Delight thyself also in the LORD: and he shall give thee the desires of thine heart. Commit thy way unto the LORD; trust also in him; and he shall bring it to pass. Psalm 37:4-5

She is more precious than jewels, and nothing you desire can compare with her. Proverbs 3:15

The Cowboy and the Irish Lass

He took a drive across the plains to clear his head and just think;
It was the beginning of fall when his emotions always seemed to cause him to sink.

Was it but a chance meeting or the opening of a new chapter in life's grand design?
Sometimes the beginning and the end are different sides of the same coin as they realign.

Her midnight hair gently blew across her face as the autumn breeze drifted by;
She had penetrating brown eyes that seemed to sparkle and dance in the light as well as hypnotize.

Having the charms of Scarlet and the sweetness of Melanie combined it seems;
This mysterious woman seemed to come to life as if from some romantic dream.

Sophistication and grace with an Irish temper thrown in for good measure;
There she stood before him in the moonlight, a true life treasure.

Hand 'n hand they strolled and spoke of their many life's adventures far and wide;
On they walked and talked as the closeness grew as now hip to hip they did stride.

The cowboy and the Irish lass came together in that fall brisk eve;
Was it kismet and was this really meant to be?

Sometimes in life fate just seems to take control and guide our steps;
I believe it's really God, nudging us back in line directing us to His best.

∼∼∼

For I know the thoughts that I think toward you, saith the Lord, thoughts of peace, and not of evil, to give you an expected end. Jeremiah 29:11

A man's heart deviseth his way: but the Lord directed his steps. Proverbs 16:9

For where your treasure is, there will your heart be also. Matthew 6:21

In whom also we have obtained an inheritance, being predestinated according to the purpose of him who worketh all things after the counsel of his own will: Ephesians 1:11

Delight thyself also in the Lord: and he shall give thee the desires of thine heart. Commit thy way unto the Lord; trust also in him; and he shall bring it to pass. Psalm 37:4-5

And we know that all things work together for good to them that love God, to them who are the called according to his purpose. Romans 8:28

But without faith it is impossible to please him: for he that cometh to God must believe that he is, and that he is a rewarder of them that diligently seek him. Hebrews 11:6

Let love be without dissimulation. Abhor that which is evil; cleave to that which is good. Romans 12:9

So now faith, hope, and love abide, these three; but the greatest of these is love. 1 Corinthians 13:13

May he grant you your heart's desire and fulfill all your plans! Psalm 20:4

Trials and Hardships

As we get older the seasons seem to come and go faster and with them, our reactions just seem to overflow;
Some emotions are tied to the past with painful feelings and memories that to this day still continue to flow.

Fall for some reason seemed to bring out those painful recollections in her the best;
Maybe because those were her most difficult trials and had seemed to always put her to the test.

She wondered deep in her heart how she was going to move on after her most recent tragic loss;
But on she must move to seek out a new future and try not to remember the high cost.

Sometimes fate seems to deal us such a terrible blow that knocks us down to our knees;
That's the time to turn to God and ask Him for the strength to get through these stormy seas.

Feel your beating heart, which says it's not your turn and you still have a mission here on earth to complete;
Just keep trusting in God to lead, guide and direct you fulfilling each and every heartbeat.

You've faced plenty of trials and hardships on this great ride we call life;
Now it's time for you to saddle up and face your new life and maybe once again to be someone loving wife.

So never give up or think of giving in, you have only just started to begin;
Pick a new course to take and maybe head west toward the setting sun and really begin again.

You will in time discover a future that is better and start to see all your dreams come true;
Just remember to thank God and trust Him to lead you each day and to get you through.

Then as sure as the sun rises in the east you'll begin to see a potential so bright and clear;

The fulfillment of your hopes and dreams will begin and you'll see a bright new future appear

∽∽∽

That the trial of your faith, being much more precious than of gold that perished, though it be tried with fire, might be found unto praise and honor and glory at the appearing of Jesus Christ: 1 Peter 1:7

Blessed is the man that endureth temptation: for when he is tried, he shall receive the crown of life, which the Lord hath promised to them that love him. James 1:12

There hath no temptation taken you but such as is common to man: but God is faithful, who will not suffer you to be tempted above that ye are able; but will with the temptation also make a way to escape, that ye may be able to bear it. 1 Corinthians 10:13

Beloved, think it not strange concerning the fiery trial which is to try you, as though some strange thing happened unto you: 1 Peter 4:12

My brethren, count it all joy when ye fall into divers temptations; Knowing this, that the trying of your faith worketh patience. But let patience have her perfect work, that ye may be perfect and entire, wanting nothing. James 1:2-4

And let us not grow weary of doing good, for in due season we will reap, if we do not give up. Galatians 6:9

Whoso findeth a wife findeth a good thing, and obtaineth favour of the Lord. Proverbs 18:22

Delight thyself also in the Lord: and he shall give thee the desires of thine heart. Commit thy way unto the Lord; trust also in him; and he shall bring it to pass. Psalm 37:4-5

For I reckon that the sufferings of this present time are not worthy to be compared with the glory which shall be revealed in us. Romans 8:18

For I know the thoughts that I think toward you, saith the Lord, thoughts of peace, and not of evil, to give you an expected end. Jeremiah 29:11

The Lord is near to the brokenhearted and saves the crushed in spirit. Psalm 34:18

A New Dream to Chase

The answer will always be no if you don't even take time to ask;
You'll always fail if you don't at least attempt the task.

You can't move forward in life without climbing a mountain or two;
You'll always find yourself in the same place in life if you don't at least attempt to.

Never give up on life's challenges and always go forward pushing on;
Then a brilliant future each day you'll see with each new dawn.

Life's not easy but it can be even harder if on living you just quit;
Wake up each day with a dream in your heart and to it always commit.

Chase that dream as far and as fast as you possibly can;
Remember this day as your new beginning where your new life really began.

One day you'll look back on your years and really grasp just how far you came;
Just keep pushing on against all odds through life's storms and torrential rains.

A smile will cross your face as you understand you're a true winner of life's race;
Then with God's help you'll realize you have yet another new dream to chase.

So into tomorrow you'll boldly ride filled with God's love, peace and grace;
You'll never stop or give in until that day when you feel God's warm embrace.

~~~

Now the God of hope fill you with all joy and peace in believing, that ye may abound in hope, through the power of the Holy Ghost. Romans 15:13

If ye abide in me, and my words abide in you, ye shall ask what ye will, and it shall be done unto you. John 15:7

Fear thou not; for I am with thee: be not dismayed; for I am thy God: I will strengthen thee; yea, I will help thee; yea, I will uphold thee with the right hand of my righteousness. Isaiah 41:10

I can do all things through Christ which strengthened me. Philippians 4:13

And let us not grow weary of doing good, for in due season we will reap, if we do not give up. Galatians 6:9

Delight thyself also in the Lord: and he shall give thee the desires of thine heart. Psalm 37:4

Behold, I will do a new thing; now it shall spring forth; shall ye not know it? I will even make a way in the wilderness, and rivers in the desert. Isaiah 43:19

Trust in the Lord with all thine heart; and lean not unto thine own understanding. In all thy ways acknowledge him, and he shall direct thy paths. Proverbs 3:5-6

Now faith is the substance of things hoped for, the evidence of things not seen. Hebrews 11:1

Face It Until You Make It

Have you noticed how some people cast a light of hope and inspiration when they enter into a room?
Then there are others who just seem to project a sense of despair and downright gloom.

What do you truly project when you enter into someplace new?
Do you project hope and joy or just carry that dark cloud around hanging over you.

Life is actually a whole lot simpler than it sometimes seems;
What you project and believe will dictate when and if you'll reach your dreams.

You can't be negative, feeling downtrodden and worrying all the time;
Don't stumble through your days like you just bit into a lime.

Your eyes and expressions will really tell what lies deep in your soul;
So sometimes you just need to face up to it until you make it and really again feel whole.

Put a smile on your face with hope and faith back in your heart;
Ask God to lead and guide you and from His ways never depart.

It's time to cowgirl or cowboy up and put a jingle back in those spurs;
Let that light within shine forth and become a messenger of hope entrepreneur.

Then one day you'll realize that you no longer need to project or outwardly pretend;
As that is who you have actually become within and you'll keep smiling until the very end.

Stand firm in the new person that you have now become this day;
Always face it 'til you make it and create the changes that you need to make along the way.

∼∼∼

Now the God of hope fill you with all joy and peace in believing, that ye may abound in hope, *Romans 15:13*

But my God shall supply all your need according to his riches in glory by Christ Jesus. *Philippians 4:19*

We are troubled on every side, yet not distressed; we are perplexed, but not in despair; *2 Corinthians 4:8*

But without faith it is impossible to please him: for he that cometh to God must believe that he is, and that he is a rewarder of them that diligently seek him. *Hebrews 11:6*

Trust in the Lord with all thine heart; and lean not unto thine own understanding. In all thy ways acknowledge him, and he shall direct thy paths. Proverbs 3:5-6

Now faith is the substance of things hoped for, the evidence of things not seen. Hebrews 11:1

Be careful for nothing; but in everything by prayer and supplication with thanksgiving let your requests be made known unto God. Philippians 4:6

But they that wait upon the Lord shall renew their strength; they shall mount up with wings as eagles; they shall run, and not be weary; and they shall walk, and not faint. Isaiah 40:31

Therefore, my beloved brethren, be ye steadfast, unmovable, always abounding in the work of the Lord, forasmuch as ye know that your labor is not in vain in the Lord. 1 Corinthians 15:58

How to Love a Woman

How should a man really show love to a woman in this day and time? A dear friend asked me as we rode along the trail;
I pondered on the question giving it some reflection and here are a few things I had to say in some detail.

After God up on high she should always come first on any earthly list;
Love her each day like only she could satisfy your unquenchable thirst.

Always put a smile on her face and place a song in her heart each day;
Hold her close at night and keep the darkness of the world at bay.

Be her protector and confidant in everything you say and everything you do;
By no means miss a chance to show and to display with word and measure, I Love You.

Don't just say it with words however but also let your actions be your real guide;
Never let her doubt your love or cause a hurtful tear drop from her beautiful eyes.

Dance in the rain together and count your many blessings both large and small;
Make each day a holiday of sorts and to her always give your all.

Give her a gentle kiss on the forehead from time to time just to let her know;
Always hold her hand and walk on the outside on the street as you go.

Open her door and pull out her chair whenever the opportunity allows you to do so;
Not because she can't but because you just love her that much and want the world to know.

Bow your head before each and every meal and take the lead saying grace;
Not just at home but in any five-star restaurants or fast food place.

Not in any way allow doubts or fears to creep into your relationship at any time;
Be open and honest about everything and take some time to read her a love rhyme.

Take her to church every week and lead her at home when the good Lord you do seek;
Always be open and honest in all that you do and say and always have a kind word when you speak.

∾∾∾

Husbands, love your wives, even as Christ also loved the church, and gave himself for it; Ephesians 5:25

But seek ye first the kingdom of God, and his righteousness; and all these things shall be added unto you. Matthew 6:33

A happy heart makes the face cheerful, but heartache crushes the spirit. Proverbs 15:13

Trust in the Lord with all your heart and lean not on your own understanding; in all your ways submit to him, and he will make your paths straight. Proverbs 3:5-6

Above all, love each other deeply, because love covers over a multitude of sins. 1 Peter 4:8

And now abide faith, hope, love, these three; but the greatest of these is love. 1 Corinthians 13:13

n everything give thanks: for this is the will of God in Christ Jesus concerning you. 1 Thessalonians 5:18

And when he had thus spoken, he took bread, and gave thanks to God in presence of them all: and when he had broken it, he began to eat. Acts 27:35

Likewise, ye husbands, dwell with them according to knowledge, giving honor unto the wife, as unto the weaker vessel, and as being heirs together of the grace of life; that your prayers be not hindered. 1 Peter 3:7

An excellent wife who can find? She is far more precious than jewels. Proverbs 31:10

How fair is thy love, my sister, my spouse! how much better is thy love than wine! and the smell of thine ointments than all spices! Song of Solomon 4:10

Enjoy life with the wife whom you love, Ecclesiastes 9:9

A Silent Prayer

There she sat by the lake remembering as those memories came flooding back in;
Oh how she missed the sound of his voice and the gentle feel of his hands upon her skin.

Time to move on and quit living on just memories through some distant haze;
The Oklahoma sun was now setting in the western horizon and the sky was all ablaze.

You feel that with each beautiful sunset that you're really just living in some ole county song;
Sometimes there are no real answers that will satisfy your mind when things go wrong.

It was time for her to put those big cowgirl chaps on and just ride baby ride;
To set new courses into the future and to the past say, Vaya Con Dios and good-bye.

Now was the time for her to get her priorities straight and to really move along;
Take down those walls she had built and let her heart find a new love song.

Put those mistakes and worries behind her and to be open to what the future may bring;
Place that smile back on her beautiful face and let her spirit let go and really sing.

So she says a silent prayer to God for guidance and strength from above;
Asking God to lead guide and direct her with His perfect love.

Into the future she now rides having given God the reins and complete control;
On the horizon she is beginning see a bright and beautiful future starting to unfold.

~~~

I thank my God upon every remembrance of you, Always in every prayer of mine for you all making request with joy, Philippians 1:3-4

To everything there is a season, and a time to every purpose under the heaven...Ecclesiastes 3:1

And be not conformed to this world: but be ye transformed by the renewing of your mind, that ye may prove what is that good, and acceptable, and perfect, will of God. Romans 12:2

Now the God of hope fill you with all joy and peace in believing, that ye may abound in hope, through the power of the Holy Ghost. Romans 15:13

Casting all your care upon him; for he careth for you. 1 Peter 5:7

Make a joyful noise unto the Lord, all ye lands. Serve the Lord with gladness: come before his presence with singing. Psalm 100:1-2

I can do all things through Christ which strengthened me. Philippians 4:13

And above all these put on love, which binds everything together in perfect harmony. Colossians 3:14

For I know the thoughts that I think toward you, saith the Lord, thoughts of peace, and not of evil, to give you an expected end. Jeremiah 29:11

But they that wait upon the Lord shall renew their strength; they shall mount up with wings as eagles; they shall run, and not be weary; and they shall walk, and not faint. Isaiah 40:31

Last First Date

Up above she heard the sound of the thunder begin to rumble in;
Deep down inside those old feelings started to come alive again.

Was a true love ever going to find her down this old dusty trail?
Were each of her relationships all destined to end in a colossal fail.

These were the thoughts that crossed her mind as she readied herself for yet another date;
Hoping and praying that maybe this was to be her last first date to make.

She heard his truck slowly come driving up her long drive;
Rushing downstairs to be there waiting when her cowboy did arrive.

This was their actual first meeting as they had only talked and texted from online;
His words were filled with loves passion and fire and seemed to be so fine.

As he walked around his truck in a Stetson, starched Wranglers with a big ole Texas smile;
Oh my, she thought as loves spark turned into a fire she knew would last a long while.

He removed his Stetson and kissing her hand gave her a single rose of white;
She took the rose and reached up and kissed his lips as loves fervor slowly took flight.

Love and excitement came alive for both of them on that dreary rainy night;
They often think back of how love and a lifelong romance on that evening did take flight.

That was so many years and white roses long ago;
Now hand n hand they ride that dusty trail, together everywhere they go.
So don't give up on true love as one day you too will find;

A devotion so pure and true with a love so strong direct from God, the Boaz kind.

∼∼∼

He loads the thick cloud with moisture; the clouds scatter his lightning. Job 37:11

... my heart may fail, but God is the strength of my heart and my portion forever. Psalm 73:26

May the God of hope fill you with all joy and peace as you trust in him, so that you may overflow with hope by the power of the Holy Spirit. Romans 15:13

Above all, keep loving one another earnestly, since love covers a multitude of sins. 1 Peter 4:8

And above all these put on love, which binds everything together in perfect harmony. Colossians 3:14

And now these three remain: faith, hope and love. But the greatest of these is love. 1 Corinthians 13:13

I am the rose of Sharon, and the lily of the valleys. Song of Solomon 2:1

Behold, what manner of love the Father hath bestowed upon us, 1 John 3:1

An excellent wife who can find? She is far more precious than jewels. Proverbs 31:10

And Ruth said, Intreat me not to leave thee, or to return from following after thee: for whither thou goest, I will go; and where thou lodges, I will lodge: thy people shall be my people, and thy God my God: Ruth 1:16

Love suffers long and is kind; love does not envy; love does not parade itself, is not puffed up; does not behave rudely, does not seek its own, is not provoked, thinks no evil; does not rejoice in iniquity, but rejoices in the truth; 1 Corinthians 13:4-6

Beloved, let us love one another, for love is of God; and everyone who loves is born of God and knows God. 1 John 4:7

Make That List

Some view fall as the end as the leaves change color and begin to drop to the ground;
I've always seen it as a new beginning where hope and a special beauty can always be found.

The changing of the seasons seems to have a major impact on people especially the fall;
Trees lose their leaves and we seem to lose some time as we turn back the clocks after all.

Autumn has a very special beauty all its own it has always seemed to me;
Beautiful changes all around both in yourself and nature if you just open your eyes to see.

It's that time of year to do some personal reflection to realize where you've really been my friend;
And to really look at your future and see what you've got planned around that next bend.

Will you be in that future you once designed when spring begins to bloom and starts to arrive;
Or will you just be traveling that same 'ole trail marking time and just trying to survive.

Now's the time to start building your plans for that future you one day want to really perceive;
Make this change of seasons a time for you to become the person you always wanted to be.

Create that list of all the things you want out of life and that you want to become one day;
Implement the changes you need to make that will help make your dreams come true, then actually pray.

Really turn things over to God above this time and let Him lead the way;
Then saddle up, cinch up and get ready to ride off into your beautiful tomorrow and for you a brand new day.

∼∼∼

Rejoicing in hope; patient in tribulation; continuing instant in prayer; Romans 12:12

Behold, I will do a new thing; now it shall spring forth; shall ye not know it? Isaiah 43:19

The eyes of your understanding being enlightened; that ye may know what is the hope of his calling. Ephesians 1:18

And whatsoever ye do in word or deed, do all in the name of the Lord Jesus, giving thanks to God and the Father by him. Colossians 3:17

For I know the thoughts that I think toward you, saith the Lord, thoughts of peace, and not of evil, to give you an expected end. Jeremiah 29:11

And let us not grow weary of doing good, for in due season we will reap, if we do not give up. Galatians 6:9

And be not conformed to this world: but be ye transformed by the renewing of your mind, that ye may prove what is that good, and acceptable, and perfect, will of God. Romans 12:2

The Lord is not slow to fulfill his promise as some count slowness, but is patient toward you, 2 Peter 3:9

But seek ye first the kingdom of God, and his righteousness; and all these things shall be added unto you. Matthew 6:33

Trust in the Lord with all thine heart; and lean not unto thine own understanding. In all thy ways acknowledge him, and he shall direct thy paths. Proverbs 3:5-6

Do not be anxious about anything, but in everything by prayer and supplication with thanksgiving let your requests be made known to God. And the peace of God, which surpasses all understanding, will guard your hearts and your minds in Christ Jesus. Philippians 4:6-7

A New Breath

She sits and wonders; how did her life come down to all this;
Her life once seemed so full of happiness, laughter, joyfulness and bliss.

It was now out of control in a tail spin, going faster down and around and around;
Then one day her world just seemed to come crashing to the ground.

Many have been there when for one reason or another, your world comes apart at the seams;
Down in flames and up in smoke there go all your hopes and dreams.

Now's not the time to give up and just think about giving in;
It's time to let go and turn to God and really give it all over to Him.

Therefore never give up on your hopes and desires or what your future could really be;
Keep pushing on and trusting God and one day He will reveal your true destiny.

No one said that life would be easy or that it would not have any challenges to bear;
Just look up and never forget that God will never abandon you and is always there.

Then one day like she had read in a poem from some old book she had been given;
Her life seemed to change for the better and a new and better life she was going to be living.

A cowboy had come into her life as if stepping from the pages of some romantic book;
With a tip of his black Stetson and a smile as big as Texas on his rugged face it had taken just one look.

Down life's trail together they now travel side by side and hand n hand together they go;

The years and memories have added up to a life of fulfilled
desires and dreams to show.

Remember as long as each day you awake and a new breath you
take;
That God's not done with you or your dreams as He will never
give up on you or forsake.

∼∼∼

*And when these things begin to come to pass, then look up, and lift up your
heads; for your redemption draweth nigh. Luke 21:28*

Casting all your care upon him; for he careth for you. 1 Peter 5:7

*Trust in the L<small>ORD</small> with all thine heart; and lean not unto thine own understanding.
Proverbs 3:5*

*For I know the thoughts that I think toward you, saith the L<small>ORD</small>, thoughts of
peace, and not of evil, to give you an expected end. Jeremiah 29:11*

*Give, and it will be given to you. Good measure, pressed down, shaken together,
running over, will be put into your lap. For with the measure you use it will be
measured back to you." Luke 6:38*

*And let us not grow weary of doing good, for in due season we will reap, if we do
not give up. Galatians 6:9*

*And we know that all things work together for good to them that love God, to
them who are the called according to his purpose. Romans 8:28*

*Fear thou not; for I am with thee: be not dismayed; for I am thy God: I will
strengthen thee; yea, I will help thee; yea, I will uphold thee with the right hand
of my righteousness. Isaiah 41:10*

*Delight thyself also in the L<small>ORD</small>: and he shall give thee the desires of thine heart.
Psalm 37:4*

*Above all, keep loving one another earnestly, since love covers a multitude of
sins. 1 Peter 4:8*

*However, let each one of you love his wife as himself, and let the wife see that
she respects her husband. Ephesians 5:33*

*Let him kiss me with the kisses of his mouth: for thy love is better than wine.
Song of Solomon 1:2*

Piercing Heartaches Dark Veil

Tears of happiness and joy crept from her soft green eyes;
Down her delicate cheeks, they flowed by the light of a distant sunrise.

A new beginning and a true love she had found at last;
It was time to put away the pain, heartache, and memories of her past.

The winds of fate can be so confusing and very fickle at times;
But when faced with another mountain she had turned to God and upward did climb.

She never gave up and kept putting her faith in God up above;
Through God, she knew he'd have to one day pass in order to be her one and only real love.

Leaving it up to God she had learned from others mistakes along life's highway;
To always pursue God and allow Him to lead and show her the right way.

Now her days were filled with love, passion, and Gods amazing grace;
Inside she now truly felt as if she had really won at life's real love's race.

It can be so uncomplicated when you put your life in God's hands up on high;
Never lose faith and trust that the desires of your heart one day you'll realize.

Then reach out and help another along life's sometimes dusty and rocky trail;
Help them to know God and to pierce through their own heartaches dark veil.

Give others a helping hand and help them back up onto their own two feet;
It's never over unless you give up, submit to your weakness and surrender giving in to defeat.

∾∾∾

I can do all things through Christ which strengthened me. Philippians 4:13

Behold, I will do a new thing; now it shall spring forth; shall ye not know it? Isaiah 43:19

Peace I leave with you, my peace I give unto you: not as the world giveth, give I unto you. Let not your heart be troubled, neither let it be afraid. John 14:27

The Lord is nigh unto them that are of a broken heart; and saveth such as be of a contrite spirit. Psalm 34:18

An excellent wife who can find? She is far more precious than jewels. Proverbs 31:10

Fear thou not; for I am with thee: be not dismayed; for I am thy God: I will strengthen thee; yea, I will help thee; yea, I will uphold thee with the right hand of my righteousness. Isaiah 41:10

And let us not grow weary of doing good, for in due season we will reap, if we do not give up. Galatians 6:9

Delight thyself also in the Lord: and he shall give thee the desires of thine heart. Psalm 37:4

I have showed you all things, how that so laboring ye ought to support the weak, and to remember the words of the Lord Jesus, how he said, It is more blessed to give than to receive. Acts 20:35

But without faith it is impossible to please him: for he that cometh to God must believe that he is, and that he is a rewarder of them that diligently seek him. Hebrews 11:6

Last Love

He awoke from the most peaceful sleep he'd had in years and slowly opened his eyes;
They're lying next to him wrapped in the morning's initial blush was he knew, life's grand prize.

Watching her peacefully sleep, her hair seemed to glow with the first light of the day;
Such a beauty she was lying there peacefully as she opened those dazzling green eyes and started to say.

Kissing her on the forehead he whispered to her, "Just rest a little while longer".
"I'll fix the coffee and then I'll be back and see about satisfying that hunger."

It had come on so fast and caught them both quite unaware;
Now here they were together and giving into this new love and beginning a fresh life without a care.

Yes, sometimes in life it all comes together like some romantic song in a dream;
They had both turned it over to God from the beginning, trusting in Him as a three-way team.

Sometimes that first love seems to hold on to us from deep within;
But nothing beats the last love that touches your heart and soul like the sound of a sweet vintage violin.

Now in each other's arms, they found love and peace they never knew;
A lasting real love that was so strong and so very rare and true.

At times in life you just need to let go and let God lead you to your fate;
God is always on time and He is never late.

So never give up and always give God and love another chance;
Don't rush or be in a hurry as your last love may be better than your first love and romance.

∾∾∾

Husbands, love your wives, even as Christ also loved the church, and gave himself for it; Ephesians 5:25

You are altogether beautiful, my darling; there is no flaw in you. Song of Solomon 4:7

Love is patient, love is kind. It does not envy, it does not boast, it is not proud. It does not dishonor others, it is not self-seeking, it is not easily angered, it keeps no record of wrongs. Love does not delight in evil but rejoices with the truth. It always protects, always trusts, always hopes, and always perseveres. Love never fails. But where there are prophecies, they will cease; where there are tongues, they will be stilled; where there is knowledge, it will pass away. 1 Corinthians 13:4-8 ESV

Above all, keep loving one another earnestly, since love covers a multitude of sins. 1 Peter 4:8

So now faith, hope, and love abide, these three; but the greatest of these is love. 1 Corinthians 13:13

Beloved, let us love one another: for love is of God; and every one that loveth is born of God, and knoweth God. 1 John 4:7

Let him kiss me with the kisses of his mouth: for thy love is better than wine. Song of Solomon 1:2

And over all these virtues put on love, which binds them all together in perfect unity. Colossians 3:14

Let all that you do be done with love. 1 Corinthians 16:14

Likewise, husbands, live with your wives in an understanding way, showing honor to the woman 1 Peter 3:7

My beloved is mine, and I am his. Song of Solomon 2:16

Her Cowgirl Ways

She'd rather be alone than lonely, the words from that ole cowboy's poem kept running through her mind;
Too many of her friends she knew that were married but still lonely all the time.

Just because you're with the one that put a ring on your hand and you said I do;
Doesn't mean he really knows and understands you and may leave you feeling forlorn and blue.

Down that lonesome trail she had traveled many times in her life;
Instead of joy and happiness, her life had been filled with loneliness and strife.

Being treated like arm candy by a man that really didn't understand her cowgirl ways;
Seemed to put them on different paths, instead of bringing them closer, it drove them further away.

Never had she felt so alone and blue when she had been married to him back then;
She had made herself a promise that she'd never go down that lonesome trail again.

Now a handsome cowboy had come into her life one bright Texas spring day;
Took her by surprise with his gentleness and charming words he had to say.

Her defenses and resistance slowly melted away as the closer she became to him;
Was it possible she wondered to really find true love at life's rodeo and a gold buckle to really win?

Then upon that moonlit ride when he reached up and lifted her down from her saddle on high;
Taking a knee he asked for her hand in marriage beneath that autumn full moon sky.

Her life was now changed for the best and words like lonely or lonesome you'll never hear her say;
She found a real cowboy on that November night that really understands her, and her cowgirl ways.

∾∾∾

Be strong and of a good courage, fear not, nor be afraid of them: for the Lord thy God, he it is that doth go with thee; he will not fail thee, nor forsake thee. Deuteronomy 31:6

Fear thou not; for I am with thee: be not dismayed; for I am thy God: I will strengthen thee; yea, I will help thee; yea, I will uphold thee with the right hand of my righteousness. Isaiah 41:10

He heals the broken in heart, and binds up their wounds. Psalm 147:3

Casting all your care upon him; for he cares for you. 1 Peter 5:7

There hath no temptation taken you but such as is common to man: but God is faithful, who will not suffer you to be tempted above that ye are able; but will with the temptation also make a way to escape, that ye may be able to bear it. 1 Corinthians 10:13

And the Lord God said, It is not good that the man should be alone; I will make him an help meet for him. Genesis 2:18

Hatred stirs up strife: but love covers all sins. Proverbs 10:12

Love is patient and kind; love does not envy or boast; it is not arrogant or rude. It does not insist on its own way; it is not irritable or resentful; it does not rejoice at wrongdoing, but rejoices with the truth. Love bears all things, believes all things, hopes all things, endures all things. Love never ends. As for prophecies, they will pass away; as for tongues, they will cease; as for knowledge, it will pass away. 1 Corinthians 13:4-8

Husbands, love your wives, even as Christ also loved the church, and gave himself for it; Ephesians 5:25

Many waters cannot quench love, neither can floods drown it. Song of Solomon 8:7

An excellent wife who can find? She is far more precious than jewels. Proverbs 31:10

And over all these virtues put on love, which binds them all together in perfect unity. Colossians 3:14

Husbands, love your wives, even as Christ also loved the church, and gave himself for it; Ephesians 5:25

Eyes to See

There are times in life when we awake seemingly without a care;
Then there are other times when the hands of fate seem to catch us completely unaware.

Life appears to be nothing but a series of circumstances down life's trail; many seemingly are out of our control;
Some we may have even caused by our own circumstances when we refuse to let go and try to take hold.

I've found it best to take life as it comes and let it just happen day by day;
To really just put my trust in Him above and just let go and let God really have His way.

When I really feel alone, lost and don't seem to know which direction to turn;
It's during these troubled times I seek out God and his presence for the answers I yearn.

We may never know why some things happen in life the way that they do;
Just keep trusting in God and many of the whys; one day He may reveal them to you.

So keep the faith, your eye on the prize and put your complete trust in God up above;
He will always be there to lead and guide you with His perfect love.

Never give up or let your fear take control of what could one day be;
Keep trusting in God and on that day He'll open up your eyes wide and then a bright future you'll have eyes to see.

On that day you'll open up your eyes to the bright magnificent new opportunities that you will perceive;
That's when all your hopes and dreams will all come together and at last maybe then you'll really believe.

∼∼∼

Casting all your care upon him; for he careth for you. 1 Peter 5:7

Beloved, believe not every spirit, but try the spirits whether they are of God: because many false prophets are gone out into the world. 1 John 4:1

Fear thou not; for I am with thee: be not dismayed; for I am thy God: I will strengthen thee; yea, I will help thee; yea, I will uphold thee with the right hand of my righteousness. Isaiah 41:10

Study to show thyself approved unto God, a workman that needs not to be ashamed, rightly dividing the word of truth. 2 Timothy 2:15

For by grace are ye saved through faith; and that not of yourselves: it is the gift of God: Not of works, lest any man should boast. Ephesians 2:8-9

Let thine eyes look right on, and let thine eyelids look straight before thee. Ponder the path of thy feet, and let all thy ways be established. Proverbs 4:25-26

And let us not grow weary of doing good, for in due season we will reap, if we do not give up. Galatians 6:9

Yet the Lord hath not given you an heart to perceive, and eyes to see, and ears to hear, unto this day. Deuteronomy 29:4

Trust in the Lord with all thine heart; and lean not unto thine own understanding. Proverbs 3:5

Delight thyself also in the Lord: and he shall give thee the desires of thine heart. Psalm 37:4

Go Chase Your Dreams

In every large city or a small country town there is a special place;
It's full of broken dreams, inventions not created, and novels unwritten by those who gave up on life's race.

Every cemetery is full of untold riches and stories that were never found or told;
Many just gave up on their dreams and died inside before they had time to get old.

Too many people sacrificed and gave their lives for your dreams and to do whatever you choose;
Don't ever give up and let their lives be in vain, ride on each day even if some days you seem to lose.

The end is sometimes nothing more than a new starting point for you to begin again;
It's that place you take your personal inventory to correct your course and then really begin.

Time to go out and fulfill your dreams and let God direct you as you travel down life's trail;
Just keep trusting in God and believe then in the end you will succeed and never fail.

So when life just throws more at you than you can handle it seems;
Time for you to cowboy up and tighten your cinch and ride on into tomorrow and go chase your dreams.

∼∼∼

Know ye not that they which run in a race run all, but one received the prize? So run, that ye may obtain.
1 Corinthians 9:24

And let us not grow weary of doing good, for in due season we will reap, if we do not give up. Galatians 6:9

For I know the thoughts that I think toward you, saith the Lord, thoughts of peace, and not of evil, to give you an expected end.
Jeremiah 29:11

Be ye strong therefore, and let not your hands be weak: for your work shall be rewarded. 2 Chronicles 15:7

Blessed is the man that endures temptation: for when he is tried, he shall receive the crown of life, which the Lord hath promised to them that love him. James 1:12

I have fought a good fight, I have finished my course, I have kept the faith: 2 Timothy 4:7

Delight thyself also in the Lord: and he shall give thee the desires of thine heart. Psalm 37:4

Commit thy way unto the Lord; trust also in him; and he shall bring it to pass. Psalm 37:5

For where your treasure is, there will your heart be also.
Matthew 6:21

All American Girl

Flaming crimson hair like an Oklahoma sunset in the fall;
Eyes that sparkle and shined and are a sky blue that seem to say, they've seen it all.

Teeth as white as south Texas cotton in the late summertime;
She has a heart as big as Texas with lips that taste like strawberry wine.

Yes this was his all American girl and she is true through and through;
All American from her Stetson hat to her boots and those were also red, white and blue.

He was her cowboy and her red blooded all American cowboy man;
She is his all American cowgirl with those long legs and a South Padre Island tan.

Together such a pair was this all American Cowgirl and Texas Cowboy;
As one they ride on side by side and so full of love and complete joy.

They had both faced life's adversities' and trials along life's dusty trail;
But on they went, year by year trusting in God that one day their dreams would prevail.

Now side by side and hand n' hand they face all adversities and challenges in life together;
They have faced many of life's storms and losses always together against all kinds of weather.

So find that man or woman that will always stand beside you through thick and thin;
Looks will fail and weight comes and goes but that true love and grit comes from deep within.

I trust ya'll will find your special someone down life's dusty trail as you follow your dreams;

Maybe God will really bless you and lead you to that special cowboy or cowgirl and make you part of a special team.

∼∼∼

Trust in the Lord with all thine heart; and lean not unto thine own understanding. Proverbs 3:5

A man of many companions may come to ruin, but there is a friend who sticks closer than a brother. Proverbs 18:24

And we know that all things work together for good to them that love God, to them who are the called according to his purpose. Romans 8:28

Fulfill ye my joy, that ye be likeminded, having the same love, being of one accord, of one mind. Philippians 2:2

For I know the thoughts that I think toward you, saith the Lord, thoughts of peace, and not of evil, to give you an expected end. Jeremiah 29:11

An excellent wife who can find? She is far more precious than jewels. Proverbs 31:10

Put on then, as God's chosen ones, holy and beloved, compassionate hearts, kindness, humility, meekness, and patience, bearing with one another and, if one has a complaint against another, forgiving each other; as the Lord has forgiven you, so you also must forgive. And above all these put on love, which binds everything together in perfect harmony. Colossians 3:12-14

Husbands, love your wives, even as Christ also loved the church, and gave himself for it; Ephesians 5:25

Fulfill ye my joy, that ye be likeminded, having the same love, being of one accord, of one mind. Philippians 2:2

And be ye kind one to another, tenderhearted, forgiving one another, even as God for Christ's sake hath forgiven you. Ephesians 4:32

Love is patient and kind; love does not envy or boast; it is not arrogant or rude. It does not insist on its own way; it is not irritable or resentful; 1 Corinthians 13:4-5

Memories of an Angel

She is his favorite memory from a long and distant past;
The true love of his life this angel fair, which for some reason was destined not to last.

Seemed so right since the very start, the moment she had touched his heart with her charms;
Marriage and a happy life had been part of their future dreams from the moment they fell into each other's arms.

Sometimes death comes calling way too soon in life it seems;
Though they both wanted to be wed death took her before they could fulfill all their dreams.

Such is life at times and all we're left with is a chorus of asking over and over "God why?"
Plus a thousand tears that even today and every day since you still cry.

They say that we'll have all the answers to our many unanswered questions in time;
Until then for some, it will be just another lonesome unfinished rhyme.

Maybe someday when he gets to heaven up above;
God will explain to him why He needed to take away his angel love.

For now, on with life, he must go with only the memories he carries deep within;
One day he knows he'll see her sitting there under that heavenly oak tree again.

So cowboy up he must if he wants to see his beautiful angel fair;
He must believe and trust in God above with every heartfelt prayer.

∼∼∼

Let all that you do be done in love. 1 Corinthians 16:14

Above all, keep loving one another earnestly, 1 Peter 4:8

So now faith, hope, and love abide, these three; but the greatest of these is love. 1 Corinthians 13:13

And God shall wipe away all tears from their eyes; and there shall be no more death, neither sorrow, nor crying, neither shall there be any more pain: for the former things are passed away. Revelation 21:4

For whether we live, we live unto the Lord; and whether we die, we die unto the Lord: whether we live therefore, or die, we are the Lord's. Romans 14:8

And we know that all things work together for good to them that love God, to them who are the called according to his purpose. Romans 8:28

Blessed are they that mourn: for they shall be comforted. Matthew 5:4

Then shall the dust return to the earth as it was: and the spirit shall return unto God who gave it. Ecclesiastes 12:7

Thou tellest my wanderings: put thou my tears into thy bottle: are they not in thy book? Psalm 56:8

Now the God of hope fill you with all joy and peace in believing, that ye may abound in hope, through the power of the Holy Ghost. Romans 15:13

Ready to Begin

He sat upon his ole horse and looked at the vistas far beyond;
Wondering to himself what new challenges may lie ahead as he pushed on.

The past years had seemed to just rock his world both to and fro;
Not much different than his younger days when he rode in the rodeo.

Sometimes life seems to throw more at you than you can stand or seem able to bare;
At times it can just leave you breathless not even wanting or seeming to really care.

From his war-filled days that had robbed him of his early days when he was a young man;
To the loves, he had lost in his life making the pain at times almost unbearable to stand.

Now once again he seemed to be at another of those crossroads in life;
Was his choice going to bring joy and happiness or trouble and strife?

If you ever find yourself at one of those crossroads of life and don't know which way to go;
Just Cowboy up and look to heaven and ask God the right way for you to show.

It may not be the easy way but to you, He'll always show you what's the best;
So keep trusting in God and ask Him for the strength to get through another life test.

Don't ever think about giving up or wonder if you should just quit and give in?
Now is the time to just put all your trust in God, cinch up and give it all to Him.

One day a special cowgirl with the bluest of eyes like a Texas sky will suddenly appear;
Then a true love, joy, and happiness will all seemingly be near with a future so clear.

Someday you'll be looking at the gold rings on her finger instead of a gold buckle you did win;
You'll just look up to thank God above for this new life that is now ready to begin.

∾∾∾

For now we see through a glass, darkly; but then face to face: now I know in part; but then shall I know even as also I am known.
1 Corinthians 13:12

For God hath not given us the spirit of fear; but of power, and of love, and of a sound mind. 2 Timothy 1:7

But they that wait upon the LORD shall renew their strength; they shall mount up with wings as eagles; they shall run, and not be weary; and they shall walk, and not faint. Isaiah 40:31

And God shall wipe away all tears from their eyes; and there shall be no more death, neither sorrow, nor crying, neither shall there be any more pain: for the former things are passed away. Revelation 21:4

Trust in the LORD with all thine heart; and lean not unto thine own understanding. Proverbs 3:5

I can do all things through Christ which strengthened me. Philippians 4:13

And let us not grow weary of doing good, for in due season we will reap, if we do not give up. Galatians 6:9

But let your adorning be the hidden person of the heart with the imperishable beauty of a gentle and quiet spirit, which in God's sight is very precious. 1 Peter 3:4 ESV

An excellent wife who can find? She is far more precious than jewels. Proverbs 31:10

And above all these put on love, which binds everything together in perfect harmony. Colossians 3:14

The LORD is my strength and my shield; my heart trusted in him, and I am helped: therefore my heart greatly rejoiced; and with my song will I praise him. Psalm 28:7

But the fruit of the Spirit is love, joy, peace, longsuffering, gentleness, goodness, faith, Galatians 5:22

Memory Slaves

Don't be the person that replays over and over the negative things that use to exist in your life;
Have a fresh perspective and a new visualization of wondrous things and let your mind's eye perceive no strife.

For if in your mind you can really see it and truly believe it deep in your heart within;
Then let God's guidance help you make this for you a rebirth of dreams and a restart to begin again.

So open up yourself and let your mind really trust in what could one day truly be;
Then the bright and glorious sparkling new future you envisioned you'll one day truly see.

Many lessons come in life and some will take a toll causing hurt and pain so learn them well;
Then the time will come to move on down the trail as you have already survived a living hell.

Now is the time to let your faith really come alive and let God and love lead you on your way;
No longer allow yourself to be just another one of those lonesome and bitter memory slaves.

Then with the rising of the morning bright sun a new day it will soon be;
Time to cowgirl up and make a new life that in your thoughts you now actually perceive.

Really now's the time to step out on conviction and maybe even give love another try;
It's time to seek out your future and fortune and take some solace in this life we call the ride.

With a big 'ole Texas smile on her beautiful face and a song of love and faith in her heart;
She was going to step out and for her a new beginning and a sparkling new and fresh start.

∾∾∾

Now the God of hope fill you with all joy and peace in believing, that ye may abound in hope, through the power of the Holy Ghost. Romans 8:28

And be not conformed to this world: but be ye transformed by the renewing of your mind, Romans 12:2

For I know the thoughts that I think toward you, saith the Lord, thoughts of peace, and not of evil, to give you an expected end. Jeremiah 29:11

All scripture is given by inspiration of God, and is profitable for doctrine, for reproof, for correction, for instruction in righteousness: 2 Timothy 3:16

I will instruct thee and teach thee in the way which thou shall go: I will guide thee with mine eye. Psalm 32:8

Trust in the Lord with all thine heart; and lean not unto thine own understanding. In all thy ways acknowledge him, and he shall direct thy paths. Proverbs 3:5-6

So you are no longer a slave, Galatians 4:7

Finally, brethren, whatsoever things are true, whatsoever things are honest, whatsoever things are just, whatsoever things are pure, whatsoever things are lovely, whatsoever things are of good report; if there be any virtue, and if there be any praise, think on these things.. Philippians 4:8

Therefore if any man be in Christ, he is a new creature: old things are passed away; behold all things are become new. 2 Corinthians 5:17

Behold, I will do a new thing; now it shall spring forth; shall ye not know it? Isaiah 43:19

Set an Example

I've seen and heard things that seem to confound me down to my very core;
People that don't realize just what they have, while seeking someone else on a distant shore.

Maybe its possessions or money they are really in search of or hope to find;
But in their foolish quest, they don't realize all that what really matters was the love they left behind.

Some seem to lose God in the process of their quest for greed and wanting more things;
They've never taken the time to stop and listen to a bird in the woods as it sings.

I guess they think that one day they can catch up to God and make it all right;
But what are you going to do and say if God comes calling today or tonight?

Each day God gives us a clean slate to write our life's story upon;
It's up to every one of us as to what we write each day as down life's highway we travel on.

So take heed but truly enjoy each and every day you have here on earth to be;
It's your life, and your choices to make so live it worry and regret free.

Never take life or those special people you know for granted each day;
Call and tell them how much you love them and not just on their birthday.

Then you won't have to look back and play the wish you had or what if game;
You will have led a life and set an example for all to emulate and proclaim.

Start today and make the necessary changes in your life to become the person you should and always wanted to be;

This is your time to step out and change all of your tomorrows that you have yet to foresee.

∼∼∼

The Lord is not slow to fulfill his promise as some count slowness, but is patient toward you, not wishing that any should perish, but that all should reach repentance. 2 Peter 3:9

And he said unto them, Take heed, and beware of covetousness: for a man's life consistent not in the abundance of the things which he possessed. Luke 12:15

Let your conversation be without covetousness; and be content with such things as ye have: Hebrews 13:5

There hath no temptation taken you but such as is common to man: but God is faithful, who will not suffer you to be tempted above that ye are able; but will with the temptation also make a way to escape, that ye may be able to bear it. 1 Corinthians 10:13

For I know the thoughts that I think toward you, saith the Lord, thoughts of peace, and not of evil, to give you an expected end. Jeremiah 29:11

Ye have not chosen me, but I have chosen you, and ordained you, that ye should go and bring forth fruit, and that your fruit should remain: that whatsoever ye shall ask of the Father in my name, he may give it you. John 15:16

Take therefore no thought for the morrow: for the morrow shall take thought for the things of itself. Sufficient unto the day is the evil thereof. Matthew 6:34

And be not conformed to this world: but be ye transformed by the renewing of your mind, that ye may prove what is that good, and acceptable, and perfect, will of God. Romans 12:2

Be careful for nothing; but in everything by prayer and supplication with thanksgiving let your requests be made known unto God. And the peace of God, which passes all understanding, shall keep your hearts and minds through Christ Jesus. Philippians 4:6-7

Missing Texas Blues

Oh, how he longed to be back where the bluebonnets bloom in the spring;
Back to that special place that always fills him with such a sweet longing.

This time of year he always seems to get those missing Texas blues;
She has always held his heart from those western plains to those eastern bayous.

Texas has always been a part of him for most of his adult life;
Saw him through good times and those years of loss and strife.

So many memories came flooding into his head when Texas came to mind where he once felt like a king;
Deep in the heart of Texas, he experienced the highs of love and the lows that true loss can bring.

It was still the only place he really ever felt he truly belonged or wanted to stay;
His mind was now made up and back to his Texas never again to stray.

What a big ole smile he had on his face as he crossed that Texas line;
He was now back home again and here he would stay for all time.

Thank you God for bringing me back home to the place I dearly love;
Here is where I'll stay 'til my dying day until you call me home above.

~~~

For, lo, the winter is past, the rain is over and gone; The flowers appear on the earth; the time of the singing of birds is come, and the voice of the turtledove is heard in our land;
Song of Solomon 2:11-12

And we know that all things work together for good to them that love God, to them who are the called according to his purpose.
Romans 8:28

And God shall wipe away all tears from their eyes; and there shall be no more death, neither sorrow, nor crying, neither shall there be any more pain: for the former things are passed away.
Revelation 21:4

But my God shall supply all your need according to his riches in glory by Christ Jesus. Philippians 4:19

Blessed is the man that endures temptation: for when he is tried, he shall receive the crown of life, which the Lord hath promised to them that love him. James 1:12

By faith he went to live in the land of promise, Hebrews 11:9

Howbeit when he, the Spirit of truth, is come, he will guide you into all truth: for he shall not speak of himself; but whatsoever he shall hear, that shall he speak: and he will show you things to come. John 16:13

For when I have brought them into the land flowing with milk and honey, Deuteronomy 31:20

Romantic Dream

As he came up the road there she stood next to the double-wide gate;
Each inside was wondering if this was love's final destination and for each love's fate.

Her long blonde hair gently blew across her beautiful face in the light breeze;
Falling back in place revealing her green eyes sparkling like the sun on a Caribbean sea.

She ran towards him as he got out of his truck and jumped into his arms, holding him tight;
Their lips touched gently at first then the flame of passion did ignite.

Gently setting her feet on the ground as he twirled her around;
She knew in her heart that her one true love she had finally found.

Up to the ranch house past the horses grazing in the pasture, they drove;
For the first time in her life, she was feeling a little out of control.

Holding his hand she led him through the double doors and said sit right here;
Then she went into the kitchen bringing back a light snack and offering him a cold beer.

Talking of their lives past and what the future for each did hold, sitting side by side;
Looking deep into his eyes she took him by the hand and said, hey cowboy lets go for a moonlit ride.

Together they rode for hours it seems both living a real to life romantic dream;
Occasionally stopping to rest and share a kiss or two beneath the full moons light beam.

The years have moved on and the stronger their love did become;

Each day they thank God that He brought them together uniting them as one.

∾∾∾

Love is patient, love is kind. It does not envy, it does not boast, it is not proud. It does not dishonor others, it is not self-seeking, it is not easily angered, it keeps no record of wrongs. Love does not delight in evil but rejoices with the truth. It always protects, always trusts, always hopes, always perseveres. Love never fails.
1 Corinthians 13:4-8

Let all that you do be done with love. 1 Corinthians 16:14

And over all these virtues put on love, which binds them all together in perfect unity. Colossians 3:14

Beloved, let us love one another: for love is of God; and every one that love is born of God, and knoweth God. 1 John 4:7

So now faith, hope, and love abide, these three; but the greatest of these is love. 1 Corinthians 13:13

Husbands, love your wives, even as Christ also loved the church, Ephesians 5:25

Above all, keep loving one another earnestly, since love covers a multitude of sins. 1 Peter 4:8

Let him kiss me with the kisses of his mouth! For your love is better than wine; Song of Solomon 1:2

You are altogether beautiful, my love; there is no flaw in you. Song of Solomon 4:7

He who finds a wife finds a good thing and obtains favor from the Lord. Proverbs 18:22

An excellent wife who can find? She is far more precious than jewels. Proverbs 31:10

Along Life's Dusty Trail

Such a beauty was she with flaming crimson hair like a Rocky Mountain sunrise in July;
Her eyes sparkled in the moonlight like a thousand diamonds shinning in the ebony midnight sky.

They had come separately from across the ocean blue and many dusty miles and even longer days;
Together they had come into each other's lives, each silently hoping the other would stay.

Closer they had come with each conversation and stolen glance they had along the way;
They were both now wearing big smiles, instead of feeling lonely and sad with each passing day.

Then came that fateful night when under the sky so big and bright;
The stars seem to align and their lips touched in a first kiss so sweet and feeling so right.

The wagon master brought them together on that beautiful fateful fall day and he was joined with his bride;
Now across the plains they go united as one, each and every day together side by side.

In concert making a new life in this new land as into loves sunset daily they travail;
Neither could have imagined in their wildest dreams that true love would find them along life's dusty trail.

You'll never know when and where that fatal love arrow may penetrate your heart within;
Just keep your faith alive and trust in God above and one day you'll feel their special touch upon your skin.

So never give up on life, Love or what could possibly one day really be;
Your new love waits just beyond the horizon so begin today and go out and start making memories.

∼∼∼

You are altogether beautiful, my darling; there is no flaw in you. Song of Solomon 4:7

She is more precious than jewels, and nothing you desire can compare with her. Proverbs 3:15

Strength and dignity are her clothing, and she laughs at the time to come. Proverbs 31:25

Ye see then how that by works a man is justified, and not by faith only. James 2:24

Let him kiss me with the kisses of his mouth: for thy love is better than wine. Song of Solomon 1:2

An excellent wife who can find? She is far more precious than jewels. The heart of her husband trusts in her, and he will have no lack of gain. She does him good, and not harm, all the days of her life. She seeks wool and flax, and works with willing hands. She is like the ships of the merchant; she brings her food from afar. ... Proverbs 31:10-31

Fear thou not; for I am with thee: be not dismayed; for I am thy God: I will strengthen thee; yea, I will help thee; yea, I will uphold thee with the right hand of my righteousness. Isaiah 41:10

Trust in the Lord with all thine heart; and lean not unto thine own understanding. In all thy ways acknowledge him, and he shall direct thy paths. Proverbs 3:5-6

Husbands, love your wives, even as Christ also loved the church, and gave himself for it;, Ephesians 5:25

Now faith is the substance of things hoped for, the evidence of things not seen. Hebrews 11:1

And let us not grow weary of doing good, for in due season we will reap, if we do not give up. Galatians 6:9

Loves Grand Prize

Back her mind drifts to when she stood on many a honky-tonk stage;
Oh, how she remembers singing and playing, driving the crowd into a musical rage.

From Vegas to Nashville and so many points along the way she did sing and play her sound;
People came from miles and miles around when she played in their town.

She seemed to have it all, a ranch, a bus, sports cars, recording studio and money to burn;
But deep inside for that one special cowboy's love did she silently still yearn.

So many times they seemed to have come so close over the many years;
Whether it was in Texas, Colorado, Vegas, Georgia or Tennessee, it just seemed to end in tears.

It seems that love's light was shining brightly as they came together this time;
Here they were as one with love in their eyes like one of those ole love rhymes.

When their eyes met and locked on one another and their lips touched sparks did fly;
You could see the passion ignite as their deep love for one another could be seen in their eyes.

We all wonder why love sometimes seems to take so much time to evolve;
Maybe it was really just us that needed that extra time to mature and grow up is all.

Now together they travel hand n hand to Vegas and so many points in between;
But now it's just for fun and love of each other and not the musical scene.

It took some time for God to open each of their minds, hearts, and eyes;
Then they both realized that before each was their destiny and loves grand prize.

∾∾∾

*You are altogether beautiful, my love; there is no flaw in you.
Song of Solomon 4:7*

*For where your treasure is, there will your heart be also.
Matthew 6:21*

Above all, love each other deeply, because love covers over a multitude of sins. 1 Peter 4:8

And over all these virtues put on love, which binds them all together in perfect unity. Colossians 3:14

Thou tellest my wanderings: put thou my tears into thy bottle: are they not in thy book? Psalm 56:8

So now faith, hope, and love abide, these three; but the greatest of these is love. 1 Corinthians 13:13

With all humility and gentleness, with patience, bearing with one another in love, Ephesians 4:2

When I was a child, I spake as a child, I understood as a child, I thought as a child: but when I became a man, I put away childish things. 1 Corinthians 13:11

*For I know the thoughts that I think toward you, saith the LORD, thoughts of peace, and not of evil, to give you an expected end.
Jeremiah 29:11*

For the vision is yet for an appointed time, but at the end it shall speak, and not lie: though it tarry, wait for it; because it will surely come, it will not tarry. Habakkuk 2:3

Delight thyself also in the LORD: and he shall give thee the desires of thine heart. Psalm 37:4

Final 8-Second Ride

He pulled down the brim of the black Stetson to block the lights from his eyes;
One final rodeo with another ranked bull, and his last outing to claim that 8-second ride.

Older than his years and he'd been around long enough to really know;
Several cowboys come to actually ride to win while others are there just for show.

His boots spurs and gloves were just right and another cowboy helped to pull the bull rope tight;
Another city and one last rodeo and he hoped an ultimate 8-second ride this night.

With a nod of his head a cowboy swung the gate open wide;
This he knew was going to be the beginning of another long nights ride.

Such is life as each new day a new life's battle does begin;
We can wake up each day and just show up or be in it to really win.

Some just take each day as it comes and try to just get by it seems;
While a select few go out to give their all and really go chase after their dreams.

So follow your dreams and let God have the reins and really let go;
Go out each day expecting another gold buckle to win and not be there just for show.

Then when the final buzzer sounds and you ride up to that big ranch way up in the sky;
You can let God know that each day you gave your all and did your best to qualify.

∼∼∼

Do your best to present yourself to God as one approved,
2 Timothy 2:15

But they that wait upon the Lord shall renew their strength; they shall mount up with wings as eagles; they shall run, and not be weary; and they shall walk, and not faint. Isaiah 40:31

The righteous cry, and the Lord hears them, and delivered them out of all their troubles. Psalm 34:17

I can do all things through Christ which strengthened me. Philippians 4:13

Watch ye, stand fast in the faith, quit you like men, be strong. 1 Corinthians 16:13

For the Lord your God is he who goes with you to fight for you against your enemies, to give you the victory.' Deuteronomy 20:4

And we know that all things work together for good to them that love God, to them who are the called according to his purpose. Romans 8:28

It is of the Lord's mercies that we are not consumed, because his compassions fail not. They are new every morning: great is thy faithfulness. Lamentations 3:22-23

For I know the thoughts that I think toward you, saith the Lord, thoughts of peace, and not of evil, to give you an expected end. Jeremiah 29:11

Blessed is the man that endureth temptation: for when he is tried, he shall receive the crown of life, which the Lord hath promised to them that love him. James 1:12

Beneath a Texas Blue Moon

He so sought to take her to a very special place, somewhere exciting and new;
Wanting so much to just get away and find someplace that would be creating a special memory for just two.

Planned and planned to make it so special and have everything just right;
How he wanted this time to be full of exceptional days and romantic nights.

Soon it would be Valentine's Day and his love and devotion to her he so wanted to show;
A romantic getaway they would go and travel north up to San Antonio.

So surprised was she and happy he could tell as they pulled into that majestic hotel;
Such a surprise for her it would be where he'd spend the time spoiling and loving her so well.

Out to see the Alamo where he told her the story of how Texas did begin and more;
She really enjoyed his lesson on history and asked for more so plans they made to explore.

Along the river that night they walked and being together was for each such a delight;
They had dinner along the river beneath the Texas stars so bright.

Sipping Texas Blue Moon Margaritas he had made for them special that was deliciously grand;
In the distance, they could hear the soft strumming of a Mariachi Band.

Each morning they would always order the same breakfast time and again;
It was a spicy version of Eggs Benedict that was so good it must have been a sin.

Later the mornings were spent at a small cafe along the waterside.

Together they would sit for hours talking and just watching the people go strolling by.

The rodeo was in town so off they went after getting her new boots in her size;
That Tennessee belle was being converted into a Texas cowgirl before his eyes.

Back to the Alamo and beneath a Texas blue moon on one knee with a yellow rose he did to her propose;
They fell more in love than either ever thought could be true and how that love continues to grow.

∾∾∾

*Behold, you are beautiful, my love, behold, you are beautiful!
Song of Solomon 4:1*

Delight yourself in the LORD, and he will give you the desires of your heart. Psalm 37:4

Let all that you do be done in love. 1 Corinthians 16:14

But the fruit of the Spirit is love, joy, peace, patience, kindness, goodness, faithfulness, Galatians 5:22

Love is patient and kind; love does not envy or boast; it is not arrogant or rude. It does not insist on its own way; it is not irritable or resentful; it does not rejoice at wrongdoing, but rejoices with the truth. Love bears all things, believes all things, hopes all things, endures all things. Love never ends. As for prophecies, they will pass away; as for tongues, they will cease; as for knowledge, it will pass away. 1 Corinthians 13:4-8

And over all these virtues put on love, which binds them all together in perfect unity. Colossians 3:14

Above all, keep loving one another earnestly, since love covers a multitude of sins. 1 Peter 4:8

And now abide faith, hope, love, these three; but the greatest of these is love. 1 Corinthians 13:13

Let him kiss me with the kisses of his mouth: for thy love is better than wine. Song of Solomon 1:2

How fair is thy love, my sister, my spouse! how much better is thy love than wine! and the smell of thine ointments than all spices! Song of Solomon 4:10

My beloved is mine, and I am his; Song of Solomon 2:16

Dreams Along Life's Highway

When you get older you can't help but look back and wonder how it went by so fast;
Back in your younger days it seemed that your youth would always last.

You now realize that you have fewer years in front of you than behind you it seems;
There is so much you still have on your forever bucket list along with those lifelong dreams.

We all think to ourselves that one day we want to accomplish those dreams or this or that;
Then one day some realize they aren't able to do some of those things as a real life fact.

Or maybe they waited till they thought that the time was going to be just right;
But along the way the love of their life was gone one lonely and sad night.

So don't put too much off till tomorrow that which you can try and achieve today;
Make every day fun to be alive and enjoy life and don't forget to make some time to play.

God didn't put us here to just work hard and toil each and every day;
He gave each of us certain gifts to use for both work and play come what may.

So search your heart and soul and see if the gifts God has given you are on display;
It's not too late to use them as you may help another and achieve your dreams along Life's Highway.

∼∼∼

Even to your old age and gray hairs, I am he, I am he who will sustain you.
I have made you and I will carry you; I will sustain you and I will rescue you. Isaiah 46:4

For I know the thoughts that I think toward you, saith the LORD, thoughts of peace, and not of evil, to give you an expected end. Jeremiah 29:11

Be ye strong therefore, and let not your hands be weak: for your work shall be rewarded. 2 Chronicles 15:7

May he give you the desire of your heart and make all your plans succeed. Psalm 20:4

Commit thy works unto the LORD, and thy thoughts shall be established. Proverbs 16:3

Without counsel purposes are disappointed: but in the multitude of counselors they are established. Proverbs 15:22

Blessed are they that mourn: for they shall be comforted. Matthew 5:4

Now faith is the substance of things hoped for, the evidence of things not seen. Hebrews 11:1

Always Keep Trying

She came to this place to find some peace and solace from her painful past;
Thinking that maybe she would figure out what had happened and why it didn't last.

Sometimes love seems so fickle she thought in her mind as the sun slowly began to set;
Maybe it wasn't love but her mistakes from the past along with some other deep seeded regrets.

We all have mishaps at times as we travel down this these trails we call life;
Some choices bring us joy and happiness while others cause us additional strife.

You can often times go back and try to change something's that somehow went wrong;
But more than likely you'll do nothing but just replay that same old sad song.

So start tomorrow with a fresh outlook and a smile on your beautiful face;
This is your new life and we all sometimes in our past did make regrettable mistakes.

It wasn't a life sentence in most cases that forever you must continue to pay;
Ask God's forgiveness for whatever you may have caused and then continue on your way.

Maybe it wasn't even your fault at all and you have no real blame;
But if you keep doing the same things over and over again it will someday drive you insane.

Look to God now and ask Him to guide your steps each and every day;
He will always steer and direct you the correct way and never lead you astray.

Now go out with the rising of the sun and let your new life really begin;
This time let God truly be your guide and no matter what may happen always keep trying.

~~~

Finally, my brethren, be strong in the Lord, and in the power of his might. Put on the whole armor of God, that ye may be able to stand against the wiles of the devil. For we wrestle not against flesh and blood, but against principalities, against powers, against the rulers of the darkness of this world, against spiritual wickedness in high places. Wherefore take unto you the whole armor of God, that ye may be able to withstand in the evil day, and having done all, to stand. Stand therefore, having your loins girt about with truth, and having on the breastplate of righteousness; And your feet shod with the preparation of the gospel of peace; Above all, taking the shield of faith, wherewith ye shall be able to quench all the fiery darts of the wicked. And take the helmet of salvation, and the sword of the Spirit, which is the word of God: Praying always with all prayer and supplication in the Spirit, and watching thereunto with all perseverance and supplication for all saints; Ephesians 6:10-18

How much better is it to get wisdom than gold! and to get understanding rather to be chosen than silver! Proverbs 16:16

Trust in the Lord with all thine heart; and lean not unto thine own understanding. In all thy ways acknowledge him, and he shall direct thy paths. Proverbs 3:5-6

If we confess our sins, he is faithful and just to forgive us our sins, and to cleanse us from all unrighteousness. 1 John 1:9

A man's heart deviseth his way: but the Lord directeth his steps. Proverbs 16:9

If we confess our sins, he is faithful and just to forgive us our sins, and to cleanse us from all unrighteousness. 1 John 1:9

For I know the thoughts that I think toward you, saith the Lord, thoughts of peace, and not of evil, to give you an expected end. Jeremiah 29:11

Delight thyself also in the Lord: and he shall give thee the desires of thine heart. Psalm 37:4

First Date...or...Life's Fate

They met one fall evening in the most unlikely of a spot;
An internet dating site, one of those single dating places you hear so much about.

They soon gave up typing for talking and his voice she finally heard;
"Oh my," she thought when she heard his first words.

The date was set and soon they will have the answer that each did wait;
Each will know if this was fate or just another first date.

She thought to herself, what have I have got to lose;
Just another friend I'll make when the date is finally through.

Of many things they did talk about, of life's many ups and downs;
What made each smile and yes the things that to each would bring a frown.

She didn't understand what was happening as she sat closer listening to his every word;
Of real cowboy men like this, she had once read about and even heard.

But could it be true, those men didn't really exist except in the pages of a romantic book;
Then she turned to him and there again was that special attentive look.

A special closeness to him she began to really feel;
In her mind all the time wondering and praying, "I hope he really is for real"?

It was time to leave and hand n' hand they walked wondering what else to say;
Suddenly pulling her close, she felt a kiss that took her breath away.

The story is yet unwritten of what they may become and if this was just another date;

Or maybe they found in each other, true love and life's fate.

~~~

For I know the thoughts that I think toward you, saith the Lord, thoughts of peace, and not of evil, to give you an expected end. Jeremiah 29:11

Love is patient and kind; love does not envy or boast; it is not arrogant or rude. It does not insist on its own way; it is not irritable or resentful; it does not rejoice at wrongdoing, but rejoices with the truth. Love bears all things, believes all things, hopes all things, endures all things. Love never ends. As for prophecies, they will pass away; as for tongues, they will cease; as for knowledge, it will pass away. 1 Corinthians 13:4-8

A faithful man shall abound with blessings: but he that makes haste to be rich shall not be innocent. Proverbs 28:20

But the fruit of the Spirit is love, joy, peace, longsuffering, gentleness, goodness, faith, Galatians 5:22

Whoso finds a wife finds a good thing, and obtained favor of the Lord. Proverbs 18:22

So now faith, hope, and love abide, these three; but the greatest of these is love. 1 Corinthians 13:13

And over all these virtues put on love, which binds them all together in perfect unity. Colossians 3:14

Above all, keep loving one another earnestly, since love covers a multitude of sins. 1 Peter 4:8

Beloved, let us love one another: for love is of God; and every one that loved is born of God, and knoweth God. 1 John 4:7

With all lowliness and meekness, with longsuffering, forbearing one another in love; Ephesians 4:2

Brand New Day

Another Wyoming sunset lit up the western horizon turning it into a glowing fire in the sky;
Sometimes this was the time of day that those same questions arose like, why God why?

We all ask that question in general but mostly we pose it to God up above;
Some things in life just seem to happen without rhyme or reason, like losing at love.

Lost love can come from many causes but the pain is still much the same;
It can come before, during or after but you still feel that deep and intense pain.

We question the decisions we made and the words we did or didn't verbalize or display;
It's now ok to let go and let God lead and guide your steps into a brighter future along the way this new day.

Not too much that this ole cowboy hasn't seen or been through down life's trail;
From experience I know this, if you put your hope, faith, and trust in God, YOU, He will never fail.

So let that fire in the sky you now perceive put a blaze in your heart to light your way;
Then with tomorrows dawn, you will be at the beginning of a fresh day and a bright new life to portray.

New tomorrows full of hopes and promises where many of your dreams become satisfied:
Days and nights filled with love and laughter and a heart full of joy that will be multiplied.

Just keep your eye on the prize and never let go of God and His perfection;
He will always see you through and be by your side and see you through every turn and new direction.

∾∾∾

And we know that all things work together for good to them that love God, to them who are the called according to his purpose. Romans 8:28

And God shall wipe away all tears from their eyes; and there shall be no more death, neither sorrow, nor crying, neither shall there be any more pain: for the former things are passed away. Revelation 21:4

And after you But the God of all grace, who hath called us unto his eternal glory by Christ Jesus, after that ye have suffered a while, make you perfect, establish, strengthen, settle you.1 Peter 5:10

Behold, we count them happy which endure. Ye have heard of the patience of Job, and have seen the end of the Lord; that the Lord is very pitiful, and of tender mercy. James 5:11

Trust in the Lord with all thine heart; and lean not unto thine own understanding. In all thy ways acknowledge him, and he shall direct thy paths. Proverbs 3:5-6

If any of you lack wisdom, let him ask of God, that gives to all men liberally, and upbraided not; and it shall be given him. James 1:5

But without faith it is impossible to please him: for he that cometh to God must believe that he is, and that he rewards them that diligently seek him. Hebrews 11:6

Now the God of hope fill you with all joy and peace in believing, that ye may abound in hope, through the power of the Holy Ghost. Romans 15:13

Brethren, I count not myself to have apprehended: but this one thing I do, forgetting those things which are behind, and reaching forth unto those things which are before, I press toward the mark for the prize of the high calling of God in Christ Jesus. Philippians 3:13-14

Sparkle of Delight

Raindrops glistened on the leaves as each droplet twinkled up on high;
He held her close as he felt her every breath and heard her every sigh.

The night before they had sat by the campfire holding each other tight;
In each other's eyes was the light of true love and the sparkle of delight.

He'd asked her to dance and around the campfire together they did twirl;
What a special time they had dancing and talking as if they were the only ones in the world.

Then it started with a soft rain touching their skin, and then it started to pour;
They continued to dance on and on till they were drenched to their very core.

Inside the camper after a while, they went to help each other to get dry;
Such a loving memory they made of dancing in the rain under a darkened rainy sky.

They will never forget how they held onto one another so very tight;
Oh how they danced in that summer rain, both feeling it was just so right.

Some memories fade with time but this memory will replay each time it rains;
How their love grew stronger that night and to this day does remain.

So never take a rainy day for granted or let romantic moments pass you by;
Go dance in the rain and hold each other tight and thank God up on high.

∾∾∾

Delight thyself also in the Lord: and he shall give thee the desires of thine heart. Commit thy way unto the Lord; trust also in him; and he shall bring it to pass. Psalm 37:4-5

For where your treasure is, there will your heart be also. Matthew 6:21

An excellent wife who can find? She is far more precious than jewels. Proverbs 31:10

Beloved, let us love one another: for love is of God; and every one that loves is born of God, and knoweth God. 1 John 4:7

Let all that you do be done in love. 1 Corinthians 16:14

A time to weep, and a time to laugh; a time to mourn, and a time to dance; Ecclesiastes 3:4

And whatsoever ye do in word or deed, do all in the name of the Lord Jesus, giving thanks to God and the Father by him. Colossians 3:17

And above all these put on love, which binds everything together in perfect harmony. Colossians 3:14

Above all, keep loving one another earnestly, since love covers a multitude of sins. 1 Peter 4:8

My Happy Place

When you feel lost or lonely and the world with its many problems seems to be crashing all around;
Think back and remember that happy place that you once found.

For some it might be on the warm sands of some distant beach;
Others, it's on that swing sitting on your front porch within easy reach.

It may have been along a dusty road with the corn reaching high into the sky;
Where you were being taught lessons that later in life you would apply.

Maybe it was a special tree that you climbed overlooking the lake below;
Teaching you unique lessons of things you could do and that helped you to grow.

We all have that happy place where occasionally our minds and memories sometimes go;
A particular place full of reminiscences and happy times from long ago.

That special place that's full of those moments that takes you back and puts a smile on your face;
It brings you closer to God and you can feel His love and amazing grace.

So close your eyes now and travel back to that particular place through space and time;
Let those blissful memories and joyful times envelop you and dance through your mind.

Now truly just let go and let God have all your troubles, worries, fears and pains;
Time for you to really Cowboy/Cowgirl up and give to God your reins.

You'll find yourself on a new life trail as God now takes the lead;
This is your life so just ride on each day with a smile and keep the faith and really believe.

And always remember that happy place you have safely locked away in your heart within.
Go back there whenever you start to feel down and need to remember why and how to begin again.

∼∼∼

Fear thou not; for I am with thee: be not dismayed; for I am thy God: I will strengthen thee; yea, I will help thee; yea, I will uphold thee with the right hand of my righteousness. Isaiah 41:10

The Lord is nigh unto them that are of a broken heart; and saveth such as be of a contrite spirit. Psalm 34:18

Let not your heart be troubled: ye believe in God, believe also in me. In my Father's house are many mansions: if it were not so, I would have told you. I go to prepare a place for you. And if I go and prepare a place for you, I will come again, and receive you unto myself; that where I am, there ye may be also. John 14:1-3

A joyful heart is good medicine, Proverbs 17:22

If I say, I will forget my complaint, I will leave off my heaviness, and comfort myself: Job 9:27

Let us therefore come boldly unto the throne of grace, that we may obtain mercy, and find grace to help in time of need. Hebrews 4:16

But by the grace of God I am what I am: and his grace which was bestowed upon me was not in vain; but I laboured more abundantly than they all: yet not I, but the grace of God which was with me. 1 Corinthians 15:10

Casting all your anxieties on him, because he cares for you. 1 Peter 5:7

Do not be anxious about anything, but in everything by prayer and supplication with thanksgiving let your requests be made known to God. And the peace of God, which surpasses all understanding, will guard your hearts and your minds in Christ Jesus. Philippians 4:6-7

Cast thy burden upon the Lord, and he shall sustain thee: he shall never suffer the righteous to be moved. Psalm 55:22

Time to Cowboy Up

The heavens seemed to just come alive with an intense fire way up high in the sky;
Was it just another Oklahoma sunset or was it all part of that long goodbye.

Hoping that this wasn't going to be another one of those extended memory filled nights;
It had been so long since he had a peaceful dreamless night filled with love and delight.

Sometimes things seem to happen in life without any correlation rhyme or reason;
Occasionally life just grows colder like the early coming of a new winter season.

Time for this ole cowboy to strike out for the west and find a new trail to follow;
To seek out his true destiny and finally put down this heavy burden and no longer feel hollow.

He needs to quit living on the past recollections of what might have been and those maybes;
Leave all those what-ifs behind or they will in the end just drive him crazy.

Needs to find that smile he use to always wear and put it back on his face;
He'll need to put a new song back in his heart, maybe one of Amazing' Grace.

Time to cowboy up and put the past where it really belongs;
Move on down that dusty trail and with the past, finally say; "Fair well and so long".

This time he's not riding alone as in the past but God rides with him each and every day;
So he'll keep trusting in God and knows that He will always show him the correct way.

∼∼∼

For I know the thoughts that I think toward you, saith the Lord, thoughts of peace, and not of evil, to give you an expected end. Jeremiah 29:11

Do not be anxious about anything, but in everything by prayer and supplication with thanksgiving let your requests be made known to God. And the peace of God, which surpasses all understanding, will guard your hearts and your minds in Christ Jesus. Philippians 4:6-7

For mine iniquities are gone over mine head: as an heavy burden they are too heavy for me. Psalm 38:4

If I say, I will forget my complaint, I will leave off my heaviness, and comfort myself: Job 9:27

Speaking to yourselves in psalms and hymns and spiritual songs, singing and making melody in your heart to the Lord; Ephesians 5:19

And of his fulness have all we received, and grace for grace. John 1:16

For I the Lord thy God will hold thy right hand, saying unto thee, Fear not; I will help thee. Isaiah 41:13

Have not I commanded thee? Be strong and of a good courage; be not afraid, neither be thou dismayed: for the Lord thy God is with thee whithersoever thou goest. Joshua 1:9

Trust in the Lord with all thine heart; and lean not unto thine own understanding. In all thy ways acknowledge him, and he shall direct thy paths. Proverbs 3:5-6

Some Cowgirls

Off she went to the mountains for some quiet time and space;
There were some past painful memories that she hoped could be erased.

Just her and her horse named Taboo at one of those horse camping venues;
No one was around and she seemed to have the area all to herself under a sky so blue.

Some cowgirls need to get away and just let their hair blow in the wind as they ride and ponder past events;
They hit replay and review them all and of the past years try and make some sense.

It all seemed to be going so well, some would say that she really had it all;
Then in an instant down she went and began an emotional freefall.

First, the loss of her husband and she still asked on some days why?
Then several disastrous relationships and a marriage that still made her cry.

Now here she was riding the trails alone and wondering what was going to be next in her life;
Her attitude she still tried to keep positive in spite of all this turmoil and strife.

Each day she rode and talked to God as she went down each and every trail;
She realized that this was only just another setback in her life, and not really a fail.

Sometimes in life things just happen and seem to be completely out of our control;
That's when you just have to cowgirl up each time and with every fall you just need to roll.

Now she was headed back down the mountain with a clear head and a fresh new perspective to match;
A little alone time with just her and God was what she had really needed to catch.

Little did she know that her whole life was about to change for the better in her life's quest;
Sometimes God just wants us to turn to him and let go so that He can give us His best.

∾∾∾

And be not conformed to this world: but be ye transformed by the renewing of your mind, that ye may prove what is that good, and acceptable, and perfect, will of God. Romans 12:2

And in the morning, rising up a great while before day, he went out, and departed into a solitary place, and there prayed. Mark 1:35

But the God of all grace, who hath called us unto his eternal glory by Christ Jesus, after that ye have suffered a while, make you perfect, establish, strengthen, settle you. 1 Peter 5:10

Be careful for nothing; but in everything by prayer and supplication with thanksgiving let your requests be made known unto God. And the peace of God, which passes all understanding, shall keep your hearts and minds through Christ Jesus. Philippians 4:6-7

And God shall wipe away all tears from their eyes; and there shall be no more death, neither sorrow, nor crying, neither shall there be any more pain: for the former things are passed away. Revelation 21:4

Casting all your care upon him; for he cares for you. 1 Peter 5:7

But my God shall supply all your need according to his riches in glory by Christ Jesus. Philippians 4:19

And whatsoever ye do in word or deed, do all in the name of the Lord Jesus, giving thanks to God and the Father by him. Colossians 3:17

Delight thyself also in the Lord: and he shall give thee the desires of thine heart. Psalm 37:4

Fear thou not; for I am with thee: be not dismayed; for I am thy God: I will strengthen thee; yea, I will help thee; yea, I will uphold thee with the right hand of my righteousness. Isaiah 41:10

For I know the thoughts that I think toward you, saith the Lord, thoughts of peace, and not of evil, to give you an expected end. Jeremiah 29:11

Chance Meeting

They had come together when each was in need of a true and trusted friend;
A seemingly chance meeting they were carried along like the freshness of a spring wind.

Into each other's lives they brought a purposeful meaning and a future so bright;
Days became brighter still, full of joy and laughter and filled with passionate nights.

From wild horses to music their conversations seemed to go on without end;
Rescuing each other from the darkness, that had enveloped them and together brought light within.

Across the plains of the west and beyond they traveled seeing the sights;
It didn't matter where they were as in each other's arms they always found delight.

The closer they became as the seasons drifted by turning into winter once again;
Now they're feelings have grown turning into a love so strong and true, each ready to give in.

Years have gone by as each obstacle they faced together with God's help from above;
Who would have believed from this chance meeting that an eternal flame would ignite into an everlasting love?

So always keep believing in your dreams and the desires of your heart;
One day you too will hold the love of your life and be ready for a new life to start.

~~~

And we know that all things work together for good to them that love God, to them who are the called according to his purpose. Romans 8:28

Now the God of hope fill you with all joy and peace in believing, that ye may abound in hope, through the power of the Holy Ghost. Romans 15:13

Let him kiss me with the kisses of his mouth: for thy love is better than wine. Song of Solomon 1:2

For where your treasure is, there will your heart be also. Matthew 6:21

But seek ye first the kingdom of God, and his righteousness; and all these things shall be added unto you. Matthew 6:33

The light shines in the darkness, and the darkness has not overcome it. John 1:5

Delight thyself also in the LORD: and he shall give thee the desires of thine heart.Psalm 37:4

An excellent wife who can find? She is far more precious than jewels. Proverbs 31:10

Love is patient and kind; love does not envy or boast; it is not arrogant or rude. It does not insist on its own way; it is not irritable or resentful; it does not rejoice at wrongdoing, but rejoices with the truth. Love bears all things, believes all things, hopes all things, endures all things. Love never ends. 1 Corinthians 13:4-8

Above all, keep loving one another earnestly, since love covers a multitude of sins. 1 Peter 4:8

Never Give Up on Love

They sat around an open pit campfire as their meal was served to them al-a-carte;
Can this and he be for real she had been thinking about their relationship from the very start?

After dinner the horses were saddled and then brought around for their evening ride;
Off on their moonlit outing with the crickets and a distant coyote the only sound and her handsome cowboy as her guide.

Her long blonde hair was gently blowing in the twilight breeze;
As her soft brown eyes captured the shooting star she now sees.

What a night it was, just like something out of a romance novel coming true;
A picture perfect setting for a western evening made for just these special two.

They soon arrived at the lake with the full moon reflecting its majestic golden glow;
He reached up and lifted her down and she felt that kiss that told her all she needed to know.

Sitting on a blanket as they watched the stars start their dance across the ebony sky;
Slowly her past memories started slipping away along with all her many questions of why?

Often times it just takes some patience and a real love for things to really work out;
Love can come gently on a spring breeze with no fan fair or like a hurricane with a great shout.

If we allow the good Lord above to direct our steps and lead us down the trail each day;
Then on a not too distant day, our eyes are opened wide and we begin to see in a new magnificent sort of way.

So never give up on love or that it can really find you anywhere you may travel down God's trail;

It may be just another celestial round as He shines down on you and sends a love that will never fail.

~~~

The Lord is my strength and my shield; my heart trusted in him, and I am helped: therefore my heart greatly rejoiceth; and with my song will I praise him. Psalm 28:7

Now faith is the substance of things hoped for, the evidence of things not seen. Hebrews 11:1

Now the God of hope fill you with all joy and peace in believing, that ye may abound in hope, through the power of the Holy Ghost. Romans 15:13

But if we hope for that we see not, then do we with patience wait for it. Romans 8:25

And above all things have fervent charity among yourselves: for charity shall cover the multitude of sins. 1 Peter 4:8

Trust in the Lord with all thine heart; and lean not unto thine own understanding. Proverbs 3:5

And let us not grow weary of doing good, for in due season we will reap, if we do not give up. Galatians 6:9

Be ye strong therefore, and let not your hands be weak: for your work shall be rewarded.2 Chronicles 15:7

So now faith, hope, and love abide, these three; but the greatest of these is love. 1 Corinthians 13:13

Beloved, let us love one another: for love is of God; and every one that loveth is born of God, and knoweth God. 1 John 4:7

Love never fails. But where there are prophecies, they will cease; where there are tongues, they will be stilled; where there is knowledge, it will pass away. 1 Corinthians 13:8

For I will be merciful to their unrighteousness, and their sins and their iniquities will I remember no more. Hebrews 8:12

God Knows Why!

He had gone to the mountains to get away and try to rekindle some of his schemes and dreams;
To have a one on one conversation with God and find his true way it seems.

We all get lost and lose our way from time to time as we travel along life's dusty trail;
Asking or needing direction and answers is not the same and giving up and to fail.

Walking with God down the tree-lined paths or climbing mountains so high;
There was just that same question that kept coming to his mind, "Why God why? He asked looking up into the sky.

God just smiled and seemed to say; "all your answers will come in time";
"Just be patient my son, one day all the answers will come or you may find them in a rhyme."

"Keep doing your best you can and all your answers will come one day;
Just never give up and I'll always be there to show you the way."

"Keep trusting and believing and keep the faith my son";
"It's now time for you to pick up the pieces and once again follow your dreams, as you're not done."

"So don't get distracted by life's many ups and downs as they come at you in life so fast;
Just keep going forward with your eye on the prize and My peace will be with you that will eternally last."

As I see the sun setting and the hand of God paints a kaleidoscope of colors in the western sky;
I know I'm never alone and it's ok with my questions because I know that God always knows the real reason why.

∼∼∼

Let us therefore come boldly unto the throne of grace, that we may obtain mercy, and find grace to help in time of need. Hebrews 4:16

But without faith it is impossible to please him: for he that cometh to God must believe that he is, and that he is a rewarder of them that diligently seek him. Hebrews 11:6

Now the God of hope fill you with all joy and peace in believing, that ye may abound in hope, through the power of the Holy Ghost. Romans 15:13

I can do all things through Christ which strengthened me. Philippians 4:13

And let us not grow weary of doing good, for in due season we will reap, if we do not give up. Galatians 6:9

For I know the thoughts that I think toward you, saith the Lord, thoughts of peace, and not of evil, to give you an expected end. Jeremiah 29:11

Have not I commanded thee? Be strong and of a good courage; be not afraid, neither be thou dismayed: for the Lord thy God is with thee whithersoever thou goest. Joshua 1:9

Let thine eyes look right on, and let thine eyelids look straight before thee. Ponder the path of thy feet, and let all thy ways be established. Proverbs 4:25-26

Casting all your care upon him; for he cares for you. 1 Peter 5:7

Let your conversation be without covetousness; and be content with such things as ye have: for he hath said, I will never leave thee, nor forsake thee. Hebrews 13:5

Trust in the Lord with all thine heart; and lean not unto thine own understanding. Proverbs 3:5

Heart and Mind Aligned

Some people ask what perfect love is and how does it actually feel?
Still, others want to know how they'll know when and if it's really real.

Look to the Bible as all of the answers about love are written there;
Keep trusting in God to show you just when and where.

Too many people rush love instead of letting God have complete control;
They try to direct how, when and where love should go.

To others it's just a physical love as they are afraid of the emotional commitment inside;
This is when some people's emotions and values crash and collide.

So ask all the right questions and take it steady and slow;
Listen to that still quiet voice of God speaking inside and He'll let you know.

Then one day with your eyes opened wide and a smile on your face;
You'll find that you're standing face to face with your true love thanks to Gods amazing grace.

So God bless ya'll down life's sometimes lonely trail, I pray true love one day you'll find;
Keep your eye on the prize and keep your heart and mind aligned.

~~~

There is no fear in love; but perfect love cast out fear: because fear hath torment. He that fears is not made perfect in love.
1 John 4:18

Love never ends. 1 Corinthians 13:8 ESV

So now faith, hope, and love abide, these three; but the greatest of these is love.1 Corinthians 13:13

Husbands, love your wives, even as Christ also loved the church, and gave himself for it; Ephesians 5:25

A soft answer turns away wrath, but a harsh word stirs up anger. Proverbs 15:1

May the God of hope fill you with all joy and peace as you trust in him, so that you may overflow with hope by the power of the Holy Spirit. Romans 15:13

Delight thyself also in the Lord: and he shall give thee the desires of thine heart. Psalm 37:4

For where your treasure is, there will your heart be also. Matthew 6:21

Let thine eyes look right on, and let thine eyelids look straight before thee. Ponder the path of thy feet, and let all thy ways be established. Proverbs 4:25-26 ESV

Amazing Grace

It is such a glorious day that God has sent our way;
Let's enjoy it as we love, laugh and play.

May we enjoy it together as if it were our last;
Let us only look forward; leaving what was in our past.

We don't know what tomorrow may hold;
We'll just look forward and into our future boldly go.

Lift up a prayer for us and star-struck lovers everywhere;
That what we feel is that special love so rare.

Then the sun will finally set on what was our past;
And tomorrow will bring us a love that will surely last.

Now into the future, we'll go feeling this love so grand;
A wonderful feeling we'll share as we walk together hand 'n hand.

Yesterday is behind us now gone with the setting of the sun;
Our lifetime of tomorrows together has just begun.

So let us not worry about what isn't;
Let us both give each other a gift of the present.

Opening it each day with care and trust praying to God up above;
May we always be this much or even more in love.

And may we always put a smile on each other's face;
And always remember that we are together because of God's Amazing Grace.

~~~

Do everything in love. 1 Corinthians 16:14

And above all these put on love, which binds everything together in perfect harmony. Colossians 3:14

Beloved, let us love one another: for love is of God; and every one that loveth is born of God, and knoweth God. 1 John 4:7

But they that wait upon the Lord shall renew their strength; they shall mount up with wings as eagles; they shall run, and not be weary; and they shall walk, and not faint. Isaiah 40:31

A man's heart devisees his way: but the Lord directed his steps. Proverbs 16:9

Love is patient, love is kind. It does not envy, it does not boast, it is not proud. It does not dishonor others, it is not self-seeking, it is not easily angered, it keeps no record of wrongs. Love does not delight in evil but rejoices with the truth. It always protects, always trusts, always hopes, and always perseveres. 1 Corinthians 13:4-7

An excellent wife who can find? She is far more precious than jewels. Proverbs 31:10

For by grace are ye saved through faith; and that not of yourselves: it is the gift of God: Not of works, lest any man should boast. Ephesians 2:8-9

She Remembered

Cotton candy clouds drifted high above as the autumn leaves floated down;
Yellow, orange and crimson leaves just seemed to cover the cold damp ground.

On she rode thinking back in her life to a happier place and time;
Back to that much more contented place in her life, when her days were so sublime.

To that place before her life started falling like these leaves in this brisk fall-like breeze;
When she seemed to have it all together and went through each day with ease.

Now the disappointments and losses just seemed to mount year after year;
Her blue eyes just seemed to overflow as the dam burst letting go a flood of tears.

Would a new opportunity come to her soon she often wondered back in the recesses of her mind?
Maybe a change of scenery would help get her head and heart realigned.

Too many heartaches and broken dreams she had already been through;
It was time for her to really cowgirl up and quit feeling so down and blue.

A new beginning with a fresh start is what she needed deep inside;
Begin again and write a new ending to this story of her life's ride.

She remembered back to the words of that cowboy's poem she once read long ago;
It was a time to give the reins over and to really let God and let go.

Time to ride back to the barn and get Misty her paint some much-needed hay;
Then it was time to make plans as tomorrow for her was going to be a fresh beginning and for her a brand new day.

You can't change the past or what has happened to you in your life;
But with God's grace, you can write a new ending and maybe still become a special cowboy's wife.

∾∾∾

Delight thyself also in the Lord: and he shall give thee the desires of thine heart. Psalm 37:4

Casting all your anxieties on him, because he cares for you. 1 Peter 5:7

But my God shall supply all your need according to his riches in glory by Christ Jesus. Philippians 4:19

For he saith, I have heard thee in a time accepted, and in the day of salvation have I succoured thee: behold, now is the accepted time; behold, now is the day of salvation. 2 Corinthians 6:2

And we know that all things work together for good to them that love God, to them who are the called according to his purpose. Romans 8:28

For I know the thoughts that I think toward you, saith the Lord, thoughts of peace, and not of evil, to give you an expected end. Jeremiah 29:11

Do not be anxious about anything, but in everything by prayer and supplication with thanksgiving let your requests be made known to God. And the peace of God, which surpasses all understanding, will guard your hearts and your minds in Christ Jesus. Philippians 4:6-7

And God shall wipe away all tears from their eyes; and there shall be no more death, neither sorrow, nor crying, neither shall there be any more pain: for the former things are passed away. Revelation 21:4

The Lord is near to the brokenhearted and saves the crushed in spirit. Psalm 34:18 ESV

Whoso findeth a wife findeth a good thing, and obtaineth favour of the Lord. Proverbs 18:22

Never Really Lose

Just like rodeo or in day to day life it takes a team to achieve and really win;
It could be those cowboys in the chutes or your loving girl praying for you again.

In the military it takes a true team to really make freedoms bell ring supreme;
Open the Bible and you will find additional groups of men making a God winning team.

Like the military, rodeo or any walk of life it takes a team to win each and every day;
To really be a winner in life you'll need God's team to help show you the right way.

Even if it's just you all alone against the world as you may sometimes feel;
Remember if you join God's team He will never be the one to yield.

You always need a good team in life whether it is work or play;
Keep in mind a good team with God leading it will always carry the day.

So it is today and was in the bible those many, many years ago;
God directed those great men and the right way He did show.

Pick your team wisely in any endeavor of life that you choose;
Give God the lead and no matter the outcome you can never really lose.

~~~

Whatever you do, work at it with all your heart, as working for the Lord, not for human masters, since you know that you will receive an inheritance from the Lord as a reward. It is the Lord Christ you are serving. Colossians 3:23-24

Let nothing be done through strife or vainglory; but in lowliness of mind let each esteem other better than themselves. Philippians 2:3

But thanks be to God, which giveth us the victory through our Lord Jesus Christ 1 Corinthians 15:57

Know ye not that they which run in a race run all, but one receiveth the prize? So run, that ye may obtain. 1 Corinthians 9:24

Two are better than one; because they have a good reward for their labor. For if they fall, the one will lift up his fellow: but woe to him that is alone when he falleth; for he hath not another to help him up. Ecclesiastes 4:9-10

Trust in the L<small>ORD</small> with all thine heart; and lean not unto thine own understanding. In all thy ways acknowledge him, and he shall direct thy paths. Proverbs 3:5-6

Seek the L<small>ORD</small> and his strength, seek his face continually. 1 Chronicles 16:11

In him we have obtained an inheritance, having been predestined according to the purpose of him who works all things according to the counsel of his will, Ephesians 1:11

Changed His Direction

He sat watching the autumn leaves catch and ride along on the gentle breeze;
Yellow, gold and crimson leaves floated on the invisible currents of air with ease.

His mind took him back through all the pain and suffering that he had seen over the years;
Back to those places and times when it all seemed to come apart along with the flood of tears.

Early on he'd learned that life really wasn't fair and over the years it had taken its toll;
There were those times that he had wondered if he'd even live long enough to get old.

He'd seen far more of his share of death and destruction it seems;
Even experiencing the loss of close family members along with his own desires and dreams.

Sometimes he felt just like giving in and giving up on life completely some days;
That's when he remembered those that had died who would love to be here now even in his haze.

That didn't make it any easier to go on but even harder on days like today;
Why him and what had he accomplished with his life except to be another corporate slave.

Time for a real change he realized and that time and place was here and now;
It was now time for him to change direction to what was in his heart and again feel that WOW.

So plans and changes he made to alter his direction in life to the one he wanted it to be;
Step out on faith and follow his heart's desire and to seek out and follow his dream.

Now he thanks God each and every day he never gave up or gave in;
He had put his trust in God and stepped out on faith so that he could fulfill his destiny and at life to really win.

∼∼∼

And not only so, but we glory in tribulations also: knowing that tribulation worketh patience; And patience, experience; and experience, hope: Romans 5:3-4

And we know that all things work together for good to them that love God, to them who are the called according to his purpose. Romans 8:28

For I know the thoughts that I think toward you, saith the Lord, thoughts of peace, and not of evil, to give you an expected end. Jeremiah 29:11

There hath no temptation taken you but such as is common to man: but God is faithful, who will not suffer you to be tempted above that ye are able; but will with the temptation also make a way to escape, that ye may be able to bear it. 1 Corinthians 10:13

Seek the Lord and his strength, seek his face continually. 1 Chronicles 16:11

And God shall wipe away all tears from their eyes; and there shall be no more death, neither sorrow, nor crying, neither shall there be any more pain: for the former things are passed away. Revelation 21:4

And let us not grow weary of doing good, for in due season we will reap, if we do not give up. Galatians 6:9

For with God nothing shall be impossible. Luke 1:37

Trust in the Lord with all thine heart; and lean not unto thine own understanding. In all thy ways acknowledge him, and he shall direct thy paths. Proverbs 3:5-6

Delight thyself also in the Lord: and he shall give thee the desires of thine heart .Psalm 37:4

Commit thy works unto the Lord, and thy thoughts shall be established. Proverbs 16:3

For still the vision awaits its appointed time; it hastens to the end—it will not lie. If it seems slow, wait for it; it will surely come; it will not delay. Habakkuk 2:3

Turquoise and Gold

The stronger she grew as time marched on, while the days turned into weeks, then into years;
No longer, she thought would she allow herself to be a captive by her own doubts and fears.

Each night she prayed to God that He'd send her some guidance from above;
And that one day soon she would again find true and lasting love.

Then as it seems to happen at times with the many mysteries of love and life;
She met a handsome cowboy who seemed to dissolve her loneliness, pain, and strife.

The words this cowboy spoke seemed to strike the right chords in her heart;
But her deep-seated pain and fear made her anxious from the very start.

So ask all the right questions and let God direct you down love's sometimes dusty trail;
If you put your trust in God and really let Him have the lead, love will never fail.

Too many times in life we appear to let our past dictate all our future plans it seems;
Then we wonder and question God, what happened to all of our schemes and many dreams.

Don't be too quick or hasty to judge someone's deeds or motives because of your past;
You may just make a wrong turn missing a diamond and a real love that would truly last.

Nightly she prayed and the more questions she asked this cowboy man;
Closer they grew as her trepidation and fear were now on its last and final stand.

No longer did she question this cowboys every motive or his many deeds;

Finally, she had decided to let it go and let God take the lead.

Now they ride love's trail together side by side they go;
With a big smile on both their faces and on each hand a band of turquoise and gold.

∽∽∽

Fear thou not; for I am with thee: be not dismayed; for I am thy God: I will strengthen thee; yea, I will help thee; yea, I will uphold thee with the right hand of my righteousness.
Isaiah 41:10

For God hath not given us the spirit of fear; but of power, and of love, and of a sound mind. 2 Timothy 1:7

Be careful for nothing; but in everything by prayer and supplication with thanksgiving let your requests be made known unto God. Philippians 4:6-7

Have not I commanded thee? Be strong and of a good courage; be not afraid, neither be thou dismayed: for the Lord thy God is with thee whithersoever thou goest. Joshua 1:9

The Lord thy God in the midst of thee is mighty; he will save, he will rejoice over thee with joy; he will rest in his love, he will joy over thee with singing. Zephaniah 3:17

Above all, keep loving one another earnestly, since love covers a multitude of sins.1 Peter 4:8

And above all these put on love, which binds everything together in perfect harmony. Colossians 3:14

So now faith, hope, and love abide, these three; but the greatest of these is love. 1 Corinthians 13:13

With all humility and gentleness, with patience, bearing with one another in love, Ephesians 4:2

Delight thyself also in the Lord: and he shall give thee the desires of thine heart. Psalm 37:4

Whoso findeth a wife findeth a good thing, and obtaineth favour of the Lord. Proverbs 18:22

Analogy of Love

She asked me about my love for her and I tried to explain;
I painted a story with words so the true meaning she might attain.

Picture if you will a single grain of sand that is equal to one part Love;
That God Himself has sent from heaven above.

Look out at that beach along the shore;
All that sand is the Love I have for you, the one I adore.

Remember that desert we crossed stretching out far and wide;
Seeing all that sand as the Love I have for you deep inside.

Visualize each and every grain of sand as equal to one part of my Love so true;
Now you can start to see just how deep for you is my Love and that, I'll always Love you.

So next time a beach or desert scene you happen to see;
Remember how much I Love you and with you I will always want to be.

~~~

Love is patient and kind; love does not envy or boast; it is not arrogant or rude. It does not insist on its own way; it is not irritable or resentful; it does not rejoice at wrongdoing, but rejoices with the truth. Love bears all things, believes all things, hopes all things, endures all things. Love never ends. As for prophecies, they will pass away; as for tongues, they will cease; as for knowledge, it will pass away. 1 Corinthians 13:4-8

Do everything in love. 1 Corinthians 16:14

A new commandment I give unto you, That ye love one another; as I have loved you, that ye also love one another. By this shall all men know that ye are my disciples, if ye have loved one to another. John 13:34-35

He that loves not knoweth not God; for God is love. 1 John 4:8

And over all these virtues put on love, which binds them all together in perfect unity. Colossians 3:14

And now abide faith, hope, love, these three; but the greatest of these is love. 1 Corinthians 13:13

Lasting Memory

From far below he could hear the sounds of the river hastening by;
He held her close watching the campfire flames as they leaped into the sky.

Softly music was playing as they talked of the many mysteries of life;
She remembered back to when on one knee he asked her to be his wife.

Many years it seems have gone by with so many hopes and dreams coming to pass;
Smiling to herself inwardly and remembering back to those that said it wouldn't last.

Standing he took her by the hand and kissing it, he asked her for this dance;
Yes, around the campfire they twirled as this was a dance of pure romance.

Around and around the fire they danced as recollections of the past just seemed to be on display;
They were making another lasting remembrance in time with each step and sway.

It's these little things we do with one another that we'll make lasting memories for all time;
Then your love grows stronger and stronger and your life becomes like a love song in rhyme.

Make each day exceptional for that one special person in your life and always thank God up above;
Being thankful that you have truly found that wonderful someone that He sent for you to love.

And that your life will become even more extraordinary as time and your blessings are magnified;
Close your eyes now and inwardly say a silent prayer that your love for each other will always outwardly testify.

∾∾∾

He who finds a wife finds a good thing, And obtains favor from the Lord. Proverbs 18:22

Husbands, love your wives, even as Christ also loved the church, and gave himself for it; Ephesians 5:25

An excellent wife who can find? She is far more precious than jewels. Proverbs 31:10

Let him kiss me with the kisses of his mouth: for thy love is better than wine. Song of Solomon 1:2

And above all things have fervent love for one another, for "love will cover a multitude of sins." 1 Peter 4:8

But above all these things put on love, which is the bond of perfection. Colossians 3:14

So now faith, hope, and love abide, these three; but the greatest of these is love. 1 Corinthians 13:13

You are altogether beautiful, my love; there is no flaw in you. Song of Solomon 4:7

How delightful is your love, my sister, my bride! How much more pleasing is your love than wine, and the fragrance of your perfume more than any spice! Song of Solomon 4:10

My beloved is mine, and I am his: Song of Solomon 2:16

The Lord bless thee, and keep thee: The Lord make his face shine upon thee, and be gracious unto thee: The Lord lift up his countenance upon thee, and give thee peace. Numbers 6:24-26

Chronic Pain

The doctors had told her that there was no real cure and they'd help her to just manage the pain;
On and on she went each day trying to deal with the intense hurt and strain.

Outwardly she would put on a happy face and just try and hide the intense pain and try not to go insane;
But deep inside being unable to do some things made her feel a certain amount of shame.

Struggling daily she really tried in her earnest to make the best of each and every day;
Some days were better but few things seemed to really make the pain go away.

She tried their drugs and some alcohol for good measure and this seemed to work for a time;
But they just dulled her senses leaving her heart wounded and feeling emotionally blind.

One really tried to understand trying to help her get through one day at a time;
But she pushed him further and further away hoping a better life he would someday find.

Sometimes life seems to throw so much at you, that you can hardly comprehend;
They just want the pain and suffering to go away, and for it to somehow just end.

So many people deal with chronic pain and illnesses and don't know where to go or how to turn it all around;
Say a silent prayer to God up above for all those suffering and that a real cure will soon be found.

~~~

And God shall wipe away all tears from their eyes; and there shall be no more death, neither sorrow, nor crying, neither shall there be any more pain: for the former things are passed away. Revelation 21:4

I will be glad and rejoice in your love, for you saw my affliction and knew the anguish of my soul. Psalm 31:7

The Lord is close to the brokenhearted and saves those who are crushed in spirit. Psalm 34:18

'He will wipe every tear from their eyes. There will be no more death or mourning or crying or pain, for the old order of things has passed away." Revelation 21:4

Is any sick among you? let him call for the elders of the church; and let them pray over him, anointing him with oil in the name of the Lord: James 5:14

He heals the broken in heart, and binds up their wounds. Psalm 147:3

Confess your faults one to another, and pray one for another, that ye may be healed. The effectual fervent prayer of a righteous man availed much. James 5:16

Heal me, O Lord, and I shall be healed; save me, and I shall be saved: for thou art my praise. Jeremiah 17:14

Blessed be God, even the Father of our Lord Jesus Christ, the Father of mercies, and the God of all comfort; Who comforted us in all our tribulation, that we may be able to comfort them which are in any trouble, by the comfort wherewith we ourselves are comforted of God. 2 Corinthians 1:3-4

Life's Ride

Sometimes memories can come pounding into your mind like the rain falling outside your door today;
Try as she might she couldn't push some of those reminiscences back in her head and hide them away.

Recollections are so often interwoven and sometimes contain both the good and the bad;
Some bring joy and happiness and then there are others that just make you feel very sad.

It takes both to really live an abundant life and make it feel complete;
You don't just live in life's valley or all alone on some mountain peak.

You'd never really appreciate the magnificent vista's you can behold from a mountaintop so high;
If you didn't climb from the valley far below and have to endure life's many battles and really try.

So here she was sorting through those past times on this rain-soaked day;
Inside she was wondering to herself why life had turned out this way.

Some things in life can't be explained and we will always be left wondering why?
Many were our own choices to make and left us with a river of tears to cry.

Then there were those times that it just seemed to be out of our control;
Try as we might want to change the outcome we just kept trying to fill an abyss of a hole.

No matter in life where you may find yourself on this day;
Just ask God to lead, guide and direct your path showing you the way.

It's never too late to make amends or to start living your life all over again;
Just put your faith and trust in God's hands and go find true love and let life's ride really begin.

Always remember that it's not how you start in life's race that really matters the most;
How and when you become the victor of Life's gold buckle because you gave it your all and never allowed yourself to just coast.

∼∼∼

But Mary kept all these things, and pondered them in her heart. Luke 2:19

I form the light and create darkness, I bring prosperity and create disaster; I, the LORD, do all these things. Isaiah 45:7

These things have I spoken unto you, that my joy might remain in you, and that your joy might be full. John 15:11

You will show me the path of life; In Your presence is fullness of joy; At Your right hand are pleasures forevermore. Psalm 16:11

Fear thou not; for I am with thee: be not dismayed; for I am thy God: I will strengthen thee; yea, I will help thee; yea, I will uphold thee with the right hand of my righteousness. Isaiah 41:10

Have not I commanded thee? Be strong and of a good courage; be not afraid, neither be thou dismayed: for the LORD thy God is with thee whithersoever thou goest. Joshua 1:9

For I know the thoughts that I think toward you, saith the LORD, thoughts of peace, and not of evil, to give you an expected end. Jeremiah 29:11

And God shall wipe away all tears from their eyes; and there shall be no more death, neither sorrow, nor crying, neither shall there be any more pain: for the former things are passed away. Revelation 21:4

Trust in the Lord with all thine heart; and lean not unto thine own understanding. In all thy ways acknowledge him, and he shall direct thy paths. Proverbs 3:5-6

Delight thyself also in the Lord: and he shall give thee the desires of thine heart. Psalm 37:4

Love is patient, love is kind. It does not envy, it does not boast, it is not proud. 1 Corinthians 13:4Blessed is the man that endures temptation: for when he is tried, he shall receive the crown of life, which the Lord hath promised to them that love him. James 1:12

Unanswered Questions

Was it a dream or a nightmare, the reality was existing somewhere in between I guess;
Life sometimes leaves you with more unrequited questions I must confess.

Unanswered questions and prayers that always leave you asking and wondering why;
The lack of real answers can cause you to become even more mystified.

That's when at times we really forget how to pray and truly feel lost;
Always remember that all your actions big or small always come with a certain cost.

This is not the time to give up on living and just throw the preverbal towel in;
Take that towel and wipe your tears away, now go and actually begin again.

Now is the time to turn to God and place all your questions and broken dreams at His feet.
He will lead guide and direct your steps making you feel once again complete.

Answers will come and broken dreams restored when you're ready and the time is right;
Maybe it'll happen during a dazzling spring day or beneath the full moons dreamy light.

You never know when your next opportunity and true destiny will collide so head west and proceed;
So always stand ready to step out on faith and follow God where ever He may lead.

Press onward letting go of the whys and countless questions from your past;
Just put your complete trust in God and you'll see a future He has prepared for you that will be unsurpassed.

~~~

Do not be anxious about anything, but in everything by prayer and supplication with thanksgiving let your requests be made known to God. Philippians 4:6

And we know that all things work together for good to them that love God, to them who are the called according to his purpose. Romans 8:28

Likewise the Spirit also helpeth our infirmities: for we know not what we should pray for as we ought: but the Spirit itself maketh intercession for us with groanings which cannot be uttered. Romans 8:26

And let us not grow weary of doing good, for in due season we will reap, if we do not give up. Galatians 6:9

The Lord is not slack concerning his promise, as some men count slackness; but is longsuffering to us-ward, not willing that any should perish, but that all should come to repentance. 2 Peter 3:9

I will instruct thee and teach thee in the way which thou shalt go: I will guide thee with mine eye. Psalm 32:8

The steps of a good man are ordered by the LORD: and he delighteth in his way. Psalm 37:23

And the LORD turned the captivity of Job, when he prayed for his friends: also the LORD gave Job twice as much as he had before. Job 42:10

Have not I commanded thee? Be strong and of a good courage; be not afraid, neither be thou dismayed: for the LORD thy God is with thee whithersoever thou goest. Joshua 1:9

For I know the thoughts that I think toward you, saith the LORD, thoughts of peace, and not of evil, to give you an expected end. Jeremiah 29:11

Stillness of Night

Upon her delicate face she's felt the gentleness of a slow falling spring rain;
She's also felt the roughness and cruelty of harsh words and how they can cause pain.

One day she said to him, "that's enough of that and this is all coming to an end this night";
"I won't go through life like this or tolerate being mistreated over and over again and constantly fight."

There was a certain amount of trepidation and fear of what now was she going to do;
But she knew inside that her faith and trust in God was going to see her through.

They parted ways as she looked up and saw a rainbow in the sky, making her feel once again alive:
She now knew that she was going to be free from her past and could really start livin' and not merely survive.

Moving on to another career away from this town and making a fresh start in this her new-fangled life;
Who knows she thought, maybe someday I'll meet my special cowboy and become his beloved wife.

So never think you're trapped in your situation and that there is no end in sight or any way out;
It's better to move on and begin anew than in the stillness of night into your pillow cry and shout.

Always seek out God and ask Him to lead, guide and direct the decisions each day that you need to make;
He never brings two people together so that one's mind and resolve the other can break.

Take some time and let your heart and spirit heal and restore themselves like new;
Spend some time with God and set a new course of action and let God lead you in what you should do.

Then set out when you're ready for the new life that you have
envisioned and planned overall;
You'll never again ride alone as God rides with you now each step
of the way and will always be there if you fall.

~~~

*A soft answer turns away wrath: but grievous words stir up anger.
Proverbs 15:1*

*Let your speech be always with grace, seasoned with salt, that ye may
know how ye ought to answer every man. Colossians 4:6*

*These six things doth the Lord hate: yea, seven are an abomination unto
him: A proud look, a lying tongue, and hands that shed innocent blood,
An heart that devises wicked imaginations, feet that be swift in running
to mischief, A false witness that speaks lies, and he that sowed discord
among brethren. Proverbs 6:16-19*

*But if the unbelieving depart, let him depart. A brother or a sister is not
under bondage in such cases: but God hath called us to peace.
1 Corinthians 7:15*

*For God hath not given us the spirit of fear; but of power, and of love,
and of a sound mind. 2 Timothy 1:7*

*Fear thou not; for I am with thee: be not dismayed; for I am thy God: I
will strengthen thee; yea, I will help thee; yea, I will uphold thee with
the right hand of my righteousness. Isaiah 41:10*

*I have set my Rainbow in the cloud, and it shall be a sign of the
covenant between me and you. Genesis 9:13*

*Delight thyself also in the Lord: and he shall give thee the desires of
thine heart. Psalm 37:4*

*Remember ye not the former things, neither consider the things of old.
Behold, I will do a new thing; now it shall spring forth; shall ye not
know it? Isaiah 43:18-19*

*Likewise, ye husbands, dwell with them according to knowledge, giving
honor unto the wife, 1 Peter 3:7*

*Howbeit when he, the Spirit of truth, is come, he will guide you into all
truth: for he shall not speak of himself; but whatsoever he shall hear,
that shall he speak: and he will show you things to come. John 16:13*

Like a Spring Rain

Sitting around the campfire his thoughts went up skyward just like the dancing flames;
Those memories sometimes came flooding back nearly driving him insane.

Both good and bad recollections were all mixed together like an Oklahoma whirlwind;
There is no good trying to separate them, as they didn't have a beginning and no end.

The pain associated with any death but especially that of a child doesn't even seem fair;
It comes with its own kind of pain that seems to take from your lungs each breath of air.

So it is with a loss of any type and the grief and pain that comes along;
You try to put on a smiling face when you hear that one special song.

The pain and grief can send you tumbling into that dark abyss that appears to have no escape or a sense of reality;
You so want to see their smiling face again and to quit questioning your own mortality.

You never quite ever get over it even with the marching on of time;
But with the grace of God, you'll get through it and not really lose your mind.

No matter the kind of loss you may have experienced in your life, just know here and now;
That God knows your deep pain and suffering and will comfort you somehow.

Cry your river of tears, yell and scream into your pillow for all the pain;
Just know that one day through it you will pass just like a spring rain.

Then someday the clouds will part and the sun again will shine warmly on your face;

So take the time you need to grieve and heal and one day God will wash over you with His Amazing Grace.

∼∼∼

And when his friends heard of it, they went out to lay hold on him: for they said, He is beside himself. Mark 3:21

Now the God of hope fill you with all joy and peace in believing, that ye may abound in hope, through the power of the Holy Ghost. Romans 15:13

Fear thou not; for I am with thee: be not dismayed; for I am thy God: I will strengthen thee; yea, I will help thee; yea, I will uphold thee with the right hand of my righteousness. Isaiah 41:10

And God shall wipe away all tears from their eyes; and there shall be no more death, neither sorrow, nor crying, neither shall there be any more pain: for the former things are passed away. Revelation 21:4

For I reckon that the sufferings of this present time are not worthy to be compared with the glory which shall be revealed in us. Romans 8:18

As one whom his mother comforted, so will I comfort you; Isaiah 66:13

Peace I leave with you, my peace I give unto you: not as the world gives, I give unto you. Let not your heart be troubled, neither let it be afraid. John 14:27

Come unto me, all ye that labor and are heavy laden, and I will give you rest. Matthew 11:28

Let us therefore come boldly unto the throne of grace that we may obtain mercy, and find grace to help in time of need. Hebrews 4:16

And God is able to make all grace abound toward you; that ye, always having all sufficiency in all things, may abound to every good work: 2 Corinthians 9:8

This Life We Call the Ride

Sometimes our lives take many twists and turns that set us on a new trail or dusty road;
Around and around like a merry-go-round we sometimes just seem to go.

I don't know where or how this new ride may one day take me;
But on I go with my eyes wide open, trusting God that He'll see me through and it's what I need.

Your journey may be short or seem at times very long and sometimes so unfair;
Just keep trusting in God as it's not over for you if you're still alive and breathing His sweet air.

So remain faithful and keep trusting in God as onward you must each day precede;
Give the reins over to God and go where and when He does now lead.

Travel into tomorrow with your heart and eyes wide open for a bright new potential He will provide;
This is your life so enjoy the passage and thank God each and every day for this life we call the ride.

Then one day your heart is going to be able to really see that once you only did in your mind visualize;
That's when on that special day standing before you is life's and loves grandest prize.

A fresh life of true love has now entered and this time it's up to the both of you, along with God making three so begin anew;
Don't let your fear or those past sorted memories hold you back that you may still carry inside of you.

Step out on your boundless faith today and let love and God truly be your one true guide;
It's time to begin a new life that was once but a dream you held dear, so sit tall in the saddle and take each day in stride.

~~~

And be not conformed to this world: but be ye transformed by the renewing of your mind, that ye may prove what is that good, and acceptable, and perfect, will of God. Romans 12:2

And we know that all things work together for good to them that love God, to them who are the called according to his purpose. Romans 8:28

Therefore if any man be in Christ, he is a new creature: old things are passed away; behold, all things are become new. 2 Corinthians 5:17

*Trust in the L*ORD *with all thine heart; and lean not unto thine own understanding. Proverbs 3:5*

*For I know the thoughts that I think toward you, saith the L*ORD*, thoughts of peace, and not of evil, to give you an expected end. Jeremiah 29:11*

Blessed is the man that endureth temptation: for when he is tried, he shall receive the crown of life, which the Lord hath promised to them that love him. James 1:12

So now faith, hope, and love abide, these three; but the greatest of these is love. 1 Corinthians 13:13

And we have known and believed the love that God hath to us. God is love; and he that dwelleth in love dwelleth in God, and God in him. 1 John 4:16

Let love be without dissimulation. Abhor that which is evil; cleave to that which is good. Romans 12:9

*There is no fear in love; but perfect love casteth out fear: because fear hath torment. He that feareth is not made perfect in love.
1 John 4:18*

With all lowliness and meekness, with longsuffering, forbearing one another in love; Ephesians 4:2

Crossroads

The autumn leaves danced on the brisk breeze high up against an azure blue sky;
Back in time went her mind to another time and place wondering once again why?

Sometimes in life, things don't quite go as we planned and can alter our life we call the ride;
That's when you have to Cowgirl Up and review your choices and once again really decide.

Things had not turned out in her life the way she had it all planned;
A troublesome relationship had left her wondering what was left and how was she going to land.

She had given her all and tried to make a life, love and their marriage complete;
He on the other hand just seemed to live for the rodeo and another chance to compete.

Now she was at that preferable crossroads where she would have to make a choice this time;
Move on or stick it out and try to make things work like she once read in a cowboy's rhyme.

Funny how our lives can get off course and send us to a place we never thought we'd be;
But here she was having to make a choice on how her life would go, not knowing what in the future she might see.

Then she saw that hawk flying way up high in that crystal blue sky;
That's when she realized it was time to cinch up, give the reins to God and just ride.

Years have since gone by and she's glad she hung on to that special cowboy man;
As several gold buckles later he is the top cowboy all across this land.

In life we never really know what may await us down the next trail;
We just have to hang on and trust in God and know that us, He'll never fail.

∽∽∽

And the Lord God said, "It is not good that man should be alone; I will make him a helper comparable to him." Genesis 2:18

Be anxious for nothing, but in everything by prayer and supplication, with thanksgiving, let your requests be made known to God; Philippians 4:6

How much better to get wisdom than gold! And to get understanding is to be chosen rather than silver. Proverbs 16:16

Without counsel purposes are disappointed: but in the multitude of counselors they are established. Proverbs 15:22

The way of a fool is right in his own eyes, but a wise man listens to advice. Proverbs 12:15

Trust in the Lord with all thine heart; and lean not unto thine own understanding. In all thy ways acknowledge him, and he shall direct thy paths. Proverbs 3:5-6

And we know that all things work together for good to them that love God, to them who are the called according to his purpose. Romans 8:28

Above all, keep loving one another earnestly, since love covers a multitude of sins. 1 Peter 4:8

And let us not grow weary of doing good, for in due season we will reap, if we do not give up. Galatians 6:9

Be ye strong therefore, and let not your hands be weak: for your work shall be rewarded. 2 Chronicles 15:7

For I know the thoughts that I think toward you, saith the Lord, thoughts of peace, and not of evil, to give you an expected end. Jeremiah 29:11

Fear not, for I am with you; be not dismayed, for I am your God; I will strengthen you, I will help you, I will uphold you with my righteous right hand. Isaiah 41:10

Heaven

Heaven is a place we all want to be;
As for now it just seems to be somewhat of a mystery.

Of heaven we cannot really understand or comprehend;
But eternity is where we all want to be someday when we face the end.

I've heard that its streets are wide and made of gold;
At least that's what as a child I was told.

I believe that heaven is such an awesome special place;
So full of love, peace and God's warm and loving embrace.

Maybe heaven is a lot like here you see;
That is, except without all the turmoil, heartache and misery.

Knowing that God created the earth for us here to exist;
So then maybe heaven is really a lot like this.

Maybe we get to live on the beach or on mountains high;
Like the song says and we get to ride a drop of rain or brush a lion's mane with no fear inside.

Hopefully, we get to see our loved ones and the place where our pets now reside;
The Bible doesn't say much, so with them into eternity I hope I'll be, side by side.

None of us really know what to expect when we get to heaven above;
Except there we will find God and His amazing love.

We can't comprehend just how amazing or how grand;
But one day if we just believe then we'll understand.

Trust in God with all your heart and His words do heed;
Then one day up to heaven and with your love to spend eternity.

~~~

But as it is written, Eye hath not seen, nor ear heard, neither have entered into the heart of man, the things which God hath prepared for them that love him. 1 Corinthians 2:9

And he showed me a pure river of water of life, clear as crystal, proceeding out of the throne of God and of the Lamb. In the midst of the street of it, and on either side of the river, was there the tree of life, which bare twelve manner of fruits, and yielded her fruit every month: and the leaves of the tree were for the healing of the nations. And there shall be no more curse: but the throne of God and of the Lamb shall be in it; and his servants shall serve him: And they shall see his face; and his name shall be in their foreheads. And there shall be no night there; and they need no candle, neither light of the sun; for the Lord God gives them light: and they shall reign forever and ever. Revelation 22:1-5

In my Father's house are many mansions: if it were not so, I would have told you. I go to prepare a place for you. John 14:2

And Jesus said unto him, Verily I say unto thee, Today shall thou be with me in paradise. Luke 23:43

Blessed are the pure in heart: for they shall see God. Matthew 5:8

And God shall wipe away all tears from their eyes; and there shall be no more death, neither sorrow, nor crying, neither shall there be any more pain: for the former things are passed away. Revelation 21:4

Nevertheless we, according to his promise, look for new heavens and a new earth, wherein dwelleth righteousness. 2 Peter 3:13

For God so loved the world, that he gave his only begotten Son, that whosoever believeth in him should not perish, but have everlasting life. John 3:16

That if thou shall confess with thy mouth the Lord Jesus, and shalt believe in thine heart that God hath raised him from the dead, thou shall be saved. For with the heart man believeth unto righteousness; and with the mouth confession is made unto salvation. For the scripture saith, whosoever believeth on him shall not be ashamed. For there is no difference between the Jew and the Greek: for the same Lord over all is rich unto all that call upon him. For whosoever shall call upon the name of the Lord shall be saved. Romans 10:9-13

Bands of Gold

Her hair was all aglow like the Oklahoma sunset seems to light up the sky on fire way up high;
Rays of the setting sun danced in her eyes making them sparkle and outwardly come alive.

She had tried to put aside her past heartache and the pain she carried deep within;
In her soul, she prayed that real true love would come and find her once again.

The walls she had built over the years reaching higher and higher seemingly into the sky;
Somehow that cowboy seemed to have penetrated them reaching into her very heart deep inside.

Before she knew it he stood at her hearts very door and she guardedly let him come inside;
His words seemed to have melted her fears and the defenses she had built over time so high.

Now she was once again wearing a real smile upon her rose petal soft gorgeous face;
Gone was the fear and worry as she was now feeling Gods amazing grace.

So never give up on love or those dreams you have carried from your very start;
Believe never letting go until that day arrives when loves arrow finds you and strikes deep within your heart.

Down life's highway you will both go and onto each other, forever tightly you'll always hold;
Then with big smiles on both of your faces and the sun will be reflecting brightly off your bands of gold.

Never give up on love or life or all the many possibilities that this ride we call life has to offer us each day;
Saddle up with faith and hope daily and vigilantly ride chasing your dreams come what may.

~~~

The Lord is close to the brokenhearted and saves those who are crushed in spirit. Psalm 34:18

For I reckon that the sufferings of this present time are not worthy to be compared with the glory which shall be revealed in us. Romans 8:18

She is more precious than jewels, and nothing you desire can compare with her. Proverbs 3:15

Be careful for nothing; but in everything by prayer and supplication with thanksgiving let your requests be made known unto God. And the peace of God, which passes all understanding, shall keep your hearts and minds through Christ Jesus. Philippians 4:6-7

Let us not become weary in doing good, for at the proper time we will reap a harvest if we do not give up. Galatians 6:9

Let him kiss me with the kisses of his mouth, for your love is more delightful than wine. Song of Solomon 1:2

Love is patient and kind; love does not envy or boast; it is not arrogant or rude. 1 Corinthians 13:4

There is no fear in love; but perfect love casteth out fear: because fear hath torment. He that feareth is not made perfect in love. We love him, because he first loved us. 1 John 4:18-19

Whoso finds a wife has found a good thing, and has obtained favor of the Lord. Proverbs 18:22

And now these three remain: faith, hope and love. But the greatest of these is love. 1 Corinthians 13:13

Above all, keep loving one another earnestly, since love covers a multitude of sins. 1 Peter 4:8 ESV

An excellent wife who can find? She is far more precious than jewels. Proverbs 31:10 ESV

Stories and Lies

Stories and lies some have learned to weave them oh so very well;
They'll put another and at times themselves through a pure living hell.

The why's, wherefores and reasons are countless as the stars it seems;
But one thing is certain that it will always be the end of someone's dreams.

Some do it out of fear for another misdeed they may have done;
Others it's just a game they play like some hell-bent dark demon.

Reasons in the end really don't matter all that much;
As the damage is already done and hits harder than any slap or such.

It's an ice cold dose of reality and betrayal that's for sure;
This kind of pain and disloyalty seems some of the toughest to endure.

Real trust and faith that you placed in them has been destroyed before your very eyes;
Most often it just leads to unforgiving words and harsh final goodbyes.

Never put yourself or another in such a dreadful and insensitive place;
Constantly do what's right and always face up to your mistakes.

It's always the cover-up, additional lies, and deceitfulness that bring it to a conclusion it seems;
Remember the golden rule and treat others as you would want to be treated, should always be your theme.

Hopefully, these aren't purposeful deeds and how you really live your life;
If so may God show you mercy as you might be headed for an eternity of everlasting strife?

∽∽∽

Wherefore putting away lying, speak every man truth with his neighbor: for we are members one of another. Ephesians 4:25

Lying lips are an abomination to the Lord, but those who act faithfully are his delight. Proverbs 12:22

Thou shalt not bear false witness against thy neighbor. Exodus 20:16

Do not lie to one another, seeing that you have put off the old self with its practices Colossians 3:9 ESV

A false witness will not go unpunished, and he who breathes out lies will perish. Proverbs 19:9

No one who practices deceit shall dwell in my house; no one who utters lies shall continue before my eyes. Psalm 101:7

The getting of treasures by a lying tongue is a fleeting vapor and a snare of death. Proverbs 21:6

Let no corrupt communication proceed out of your mouth, but that which is good to the use of edifying, that it may minister grace unto the hearers. Ephesians 4:29

A true witness deliverers souls: but a deceitful witness speaks lies. Proverbs 14:25

A righteous man hates lying: but a wicked man is loathsome, and cometh to shame. Proverbs 13:5

Marriage is honorable in all, and the bed undefiled: but whoremongers and adulterers God will judge. Hebrews 13:4

The lip of truth shall be established for ever: but a lying tongue is but for a moment. Proverbs 12:19

Cinch Up, Never Give Up

He sat on his ole horse and looked at the distant vistas far beyond;
Wondering to himself what challenges might lay ahead with life as he pushed on.

The past years really seemed to have rocked his world both to and fro;
Just like back in his younger days when he rode in the rodeo.

Sometimes life seems to throw more at you than you can stand or even seem to bare;
It can just leave you breathless not really feeling or wanting to care.

From the war-filled days that had robbed him of his very youth when he was not yet even a man;
To the many losses, he'd faced in life making the pain almost unbearable to stand.

Now once again here he was at another of those crossroads that we all face in life;
Was this the time he was going to find joy and happiness or just more trouble and strife.

So if you find yourself at one of those crossroads in life and don't know which way to go;
Time to cowboy up, look to heaven and ask God for the right way for you to show.

It may not be the easiest of ways, but to you, He'll always show you the very best;
Cinch up and just keep trusting in God and pray for additional strength to get through each test.

Then one day a beautiful cowgirl with the bluest eyes like a Texas fall sky will suddenly appear;
A true love, joy, and happiness will all become so crystal clear and now they are also very near.

Never think of giving up or even consider just calling it quits and giving in;
Put all your faith and trust in God above and truly give it all over to him.

Then one day you'll look back and realize that it wasn't the gold buckle but a gold ring you did win;
You'll thank God each day for this new life as the two of you go together hand n hand ready to begin.

~~~

Consider it pure joy, my brothers and sisters, whenever you face trials of many kinds, because you know that the testing of your faith produces perseverance. Let perseverance finish its work so that you may be mature and complete, not lacking anything. James 1:2-4

Be anxious for nothing, but in everything by prayer and supplication, with thanksgiving, let your requests be made known to God; Philippians 4:6

We are troubled on every side, yet not distressed; we are perplexed, but not in despair; Persecuted but not forsaken; cast down, but not destroyed; 2 Corinthians 4:8-9

I can do all things through Christ which strengthened me. Philippians 4:13

These things I have spoken unto you, that in me ye might have peace. In the world ye shall have tribulation: but be of good cheer; I have overcome the world. John 16:33

Teach me good judgment and knowledge: for I have believed thy commandments. Psalm 119:66

And God shall wipe away all tears from their eyes; and there shall be no more death, neither sorrow, nor crying, neither shall there be any more pain: for the former things are passed away. Revelation 21:4

For I reckon that the sufferings of this present time are not worthy to be compared with the glory which shall be revealed in us. Romans 8:18

For I know the thoughts that I think toward you, saith the Lord, thoughts of peace, and not of evil, to give you an expected end. Jeremiah 29:11

And let us not grow weary of doing good, for in due season we will reap, if we do not give up. Galatians 6:9

Fear thou not; for I am with thee: be not dismayed; for I am thy God: I will strengthen thee; yea, I will help thee; yea, I will uphold thee with the right hand of my righteousness. Isaiah 41:10

Her Independence Day

The blackness and stillness of the night was suddenly illuminated by the fireworks high in the air;
This was going to be a fresh beginning for her and a new life without all her past cares.

Now each rocket was soaring up streaming light with golden droplets into the darkened sky;
Each rocket seemed to burst away all her wonderings and asking questions like, "why God why".

She realized that with each new explosion of light in the darkened sky up high above;
That this was going to be a new life for her and she would find that perfect love.

With each new explosion in the skies, it seemed to settle all her doubts and fears deep inside;
This was her Independence Day and for her the foundation of a new life that God would provide.

Now she looks forward to each new dawn with the rising sun and the promises it will bring;
In her heart, God has filled it with a special peace and a new love song to sing.

So next time you see those fireworks bursting way up so high, this is also you're Independence Day;
Remember who's really in charge and knows your hopes, dreams and all the secrets you hide away.

So bow your head and say a prayer for all the new beginnings and fresh starts out there;
Then saddle up and into your bright new future, Ride Cowgirl Ride, and on your lips always a silent prayer.

~~~

For I know the thoughts that I think toward you, saith the Lord, thoughts of peace, and not of evil, to give you an expected end. Jeremiah 29:11

Behold, thou desires truth in the inward parts: and in the hidden part thou shall make me to know wisdom. Psalm 51:6

May he give you the desire of your heart and make all your plans succeed. Psalm 20:4

Come unto me, all ye that labor and are heavy laden, and I will give you rest. Take my yoke upon you, and learn of me; for I am meek and lowly in heart: and ye shall find rest unto your souls. For my yoke is easy, and my burden is light. Matthew 11:28-30

There is no fear in love, but perfect love casts out fear. For fear has to do with punishment, and whoever fears has not been perfected in love. 1 John 4:18

Above all, keep loving one another earnestly, since love covers a multitude of sins. 1 Peter 4:8

Fear thou not; for I am with thee: be not dismayed; for I am thy God: I will strengthen thee; yea, I will help thee; yea, I will uphold thee with the right hand of my righteousness. Isaiah 41:10

For God hath not given us the spirit of fear; but of power, and of love, and of a sound mind. 2 Timothy 1:7

Create in me a clean heart, O God; and renew a right spirit within me. Psalm 51:10

But my God shall supply all your needs according to his riches in glory by Christ Jesus. Philippians 4:19

Her Sweet Sweet Love

I told her that to the beach we would go tomorrow and just have some fun and play;
We'll get an early start and make it an especially fun and enjoyable day.

It was such a beautiful spring day, so off to South Padre Island we did drive;
Taking our time we talked about so many things with her sitting close by my side.

There was a special store I had in mind that I very much wanted her to see;
It would be the first time that for each of us to go there and what a place it was said to be.

The store I knew would give her such joy and a special child like delight;
For I had in mind to buy for her a very special high flying kite.

We looked and we looked as there were so many choices from which to buy;
Flashing that charming smile of hers she asked the clerk, in this wind are they very hard to fly?

Then she saw the one she wanted and of course, it was hanging up on the ceiling so very high above;
Towering up so very high was a 40-foot green dragon kite, she would later name Puff with love.

I purchased the kite and accessories and now off to the beach we were on our way;
The next stop was to purchase a special picnic lunch for later in the day.

So out onto the beach and up north on the island, we did drive;
She was like a child so excited and wanted so much to see Puff fly.

Driving through the sand until we found our particular spot miles up along the northeastern shore;
It was our special place we had traveled too so many times before.

Playfully we ate our lunch and talked about our hopes, dreams and of this exceptional love we had found;
Then it was time for her to let Puff take flight and soar high up above the sandy ground.

I assembled Puff with great skill and lots of tender loving care;
Now it was time for this great green dragon to come alive and really take to the skies high up into the air.

Up Puff flew higher and higher into the bright crystal blue Texas sky;
How majestic he looked flying high and what a twinkle she had sparkling in her eyes.

"I'd like to fly like that when I get to heaven, think I can fly like an angel high up above?"
Now she truly soars with the angels and watches over me from heaven above sending down her sweet sweet love.

~~~

Let all that you do be done in love. 1 Corinthians 16:14

Anyone who does not love does not know God, because God is love. 1 John 4:8

And above all these put on love, which binds everything together in perfect harmony. Colossians 3:14

Above all, keep loving one another earnestly, since love covers a multitude of sins. 1 Peter 4:8

So now faith, hope, and love abide, these three; but the greatest of these is love. 1 Corinthians 13:13

Beloved, let us love one another: for love is of God; and every one that loveth is born of God, and knoweth God. 1 John 4:7 ESV

There is no fear in love, but perfect love casts out fear. For fear has to do with punishment, and whoever fears has not been perfected in love. We love because he first loved us. 1 John 4:18-19

Set me as a seal upon thine heart, as a seal upon thine arm: for love is strong as death; jealousy is cruel as the grave: Song of Solomon 8:6

And the Lord God said, It is not good that the man should be alone; I will make him an help meet for him. Genesis 2:18

Let him kiss me with the kisses of his mouth: for thy love is better than wine. Song of Solomon 1:2
His mouth is most sweet: yea, he is altogether lovely. This is my beloved, Song of Solomon 5:16

Talk and Listen to God

The quiet and stillness of the mountains sometimes can make things seem so very clear;
The fresh air and sky so blue seem to be as if God is standing there with you and so near.

You can almost hear Him speak to you in the stillness of the star-filled night;
He just seems to envelop you in a heavenly hug of pure love that seems so right.

Go to the mountains, desert or distant plains of this great and wonderful land;
Sit quietly and listen and you will hear Him deep inside and feel the loving presence of his almighty hand.

Spend some quiet time talking to God just like a trusted friend in the stillness of a new day;
Now just sit back and listen and you will begin to hear what He has to say.

This is really nothing new as people have been doing it since the dawn of time;
We've just have gotten so busy in our daily lives we just seem to forget how to pray and unwind.

So clear your calendars, minds, and hearts and go spend some time in the great outdoors;
Talk and listen to God on high and who knows you might even see an eagle soar.

~~~

And this is the confidence that we have in him that, if we ask any thing according to his will, he hears us: 1 John 5:14 ESV

He that is of God hears God's words: ye therefore hear them not, John 8:47

And if we know that he hear us, whatsoever we ask, we know that we have the petitions that we desired of him. 1 John 5:15

My sheep hear my voice, and I know them, and they follow me. I give them eternal life, and they will never perish, and no one will snatch them out of my hand. John 10:27-28

And he said unto them, Take heed what ye hear: with what measure ye mete, it shall be measured to you: and unto you that hear shall more be given .Mark 4:24

Call unto me, and I will answer thee, and show thee great and mighty things, which thou knows not. Jeremiah 33:3

But they that wait upon the Lord shall renew their strength; they shall mount up with wings as eagles; they shall run, and not be weary; and they shall walk, and not faint. Isaiah 40:31

But he answered, "It is written, "'Man shall not live by bread alone, but by every word that comes from the mouth of God.'" Matthew 4:4

Listen to advice and accept instruction, that you may gain wisdom in the future. Proverbs 19:20

Her Mustang Ways

I set out to tame that little ole' mustang and make her all mine;
Then she laid those ears back and took me on the ride of a lifetime.

After a while she seemed to settle down and together we fit into a stride;
It turned into one of this ole cowboy's fondest rides.

Now together they go across each pasture and hill;
Inside each of them is actually once again beginning to really feel.

As the ride goes on the closer they have become;
All fear is gone and to his velvet hands, she did succumb.

Now each and every day off they go for another long ride;
They have both settled down into a rhythm like an old love rhyme.

That ole cowboy it seems is the one who was really settled and tamed;
Her Mustang ways really took him by surprise as at his heart she had taken aim.

So it is with life and love it sometimes seems;
Enjoy this life we call the ride and always go in search of your dreams.

The true love of your life could be found down that trail that you are now bound;
Saddle up and head west and seek out your true loves quest until she is found.

∼∼∼

Delight thyself also in the Lord: and he shall give thee the desires of thine heart. Commit thy way unto the Lord; trust also in him; and he shall bring it to pass. Psalm 37:4-5

If ye abide in me, and my words abide in you, ye shall ask what ye will, and it shall be done unto you. John 15:7

Then shalt thou delight thyself in the Lord; and I will cause thee to ride upon the high places of the earth, and feed thee with the heritage of Jacob thy father: for the mouth of the Lord hath spoken it. Isaiah 58:14

Love is patient and kind; love does not envy or boast; it is not arrogant or rude. It does not insist on its own way; it is not irritable or resentful; it does not rejoice at wrongdoing, but rejoices with the truth. Love bears all things, believes all things, hopes all things, endures all things. Love never ends. As for prophecies, they will pass away; as for tongues, they will cease; as for knowledge, it will pass away. 1 Corinthians 13:4-8

He who finds a wife finds what is good and receives favor from the Lord. Proverbs 18:22

Above all, keep loving one another earnestly, since love covers a multitude of sins. 1 Peter 4:8

And now abide faith, hope, love, these three; but the greatest of these is love. 1 Corinthians 13:13

Texas Cowboy and a Tennessee Lady

Amberjacks on the Laguna Madre is the place she loved the best;
There they would often sit on the deck and watch another magnificent sunset.

So much fun they always had sharing life's stories while laughing and smiling;
Then after dinner they'd would always just go walking and talking.

They would stroll along the bay and watch the Texas stars shining so bright above;
Everyone would always notice and could tell just how much they were in love.

Stopping at times she would say, "smooch break" along the way;
Never did they really care if it was an affectionate public display.

This cowboy and lady made such an impression as they walked expressing their devotion to one another.
Along the water, they did stroll she was his women and he was her love like no other.

They were so much in love with each other and didn't really seem to care;
All over and any place they went all around them love seemed to always be in the air.

Everywhere seemed to be their special place and hand 'n hand they could always be found;
When they were together there were always smiles on their faces and never a frown.

A Texas Cowboy and a Tennessee Lady are still talked about on South Padre Island to this very day;
That special couple whose true love for one another was always shining bright and on display.

∾∾∾

If I speak in the tongues of men and of angels, but have not love, I am a noisy gong or a clanging cymbal. And if I have prophetic powers, and understand all mysteries and all knowledge, and if I have all faith, so as to remove mountains, but have not love, I am nothing. If I give away all I have, and if I deliver up my body to be burned, but have not love, I gain nothing. Love is patient and kind; love does not envy or boast; it is not arrogant or rude. It does not insist on its own way; it is not irritable or resentful; .. 1 Corinthians 13:1-13

And above all these put on love, which binds everything together in perfect harmony. Colossians 3:14

Let him kiss me with the kisses of his mouth! For your love is better than wine; Song of Solomon 1:2

Beloved, let us love one another: for love is of God; and every one that loves is born of God, and knoweth God. 1 John 4:7

We love because he first loved us. 1 John 4:19

Let all that you do be done in love. 1 Corinthians 16:14

Many waters cannot quench love, neither can floods drown it. Song of Solomon 8:7

Let not steadfast love and faithfulness forsake you; bind them around your neck; write them on the tablet of your heart. Proverbs 3:3-4

And we know that for those who love God all things work together for good, for those who are called according to his purpose. Romans 8:28

Begin Again

He's been through the pain and suffering that most he prays will never know;
Felt so down once he didn't even have the strength to get off the floor and go.

He'd been beaten so low and was constantly flooded with wars memories as they replayed;
There didn't seem to be an escape and he could no longer find the words to pray.

Lower he seemed to plummet as with each passing day the more he drank;
Down and down he seemed to go, around n round till it all just went blank.

He heard that amazing voice and then saw a magnificent glorious light;
"It's not your time my son", the voice seem to say, "Not on this night".

"For you my son I still have plans and a life you've yet to see;
So don't give up just take my hand and you I will lead".

Then he awoke drenched in sweat, just he and the gun lying there on the bed;
He had come so close but God had intervened and he was not dead.

It was as if those dark clouds in his mind had parted and he was able to really clearly see;
No more of the shadows and despair but an illuminated bright future leading to his real destiny.

Looking back now, how had he fallen down so far and to feel so lost, alone and low?
How had he gotten to the point of utter desolation with no hope and nowhere to go?

It took some time and the help of friends who have been there, but it also seemed to happen so fast;
No longer was his lonely nights filled with despair, but new hope and a beginning he knew would last.

So never give up and call it quits or throw life's towel in;
Now's the time to really Cowboy Up and turn it over to God and really begin again.

Don't let the loneliness and despair drag you down to that dark abyss where it is so hard to escape;
Reach out to friends, family, and God above as it's never too late for your life to reshape.

∼∼∼

These things I have spoken unto you, that in me ye might have peace. In the world ye shall have tribulation: but be of good cheer; I have overcome the world. John 16:33

But the God of all grace, who hath called us unto his eternal glory by Christ Jesus, after that ye have suffered a while, make you perfect, establish, strengthen, settle you. 1 Peter 5:10

And God shall wipe away all tears from their eyes; and there shall be no more death, neither sorrow, nor crying, neither shall there be any more pain: for the former things are passed away. Revelation 21:4

For God, who said, "Let light shine out of darkness," has shown in our hearts to give the light of the knowledge of the glory of God in the face of Jesus Christ. 2 Corinthians 4:6

And we know that all things work together for good to them that love God, to them who are the called according to his purpose. Romans 8:28

For I know the thoughts that I think toward you, saith the Lord, thoughts of peace, and not of evil, to give you an expected end. Jeremiah 29:11

Fear thou not; for I am with thee: be not dismayed; for I am thy God: I will strengthen thee; yea, I will help thee; yea, I will uphold thee with the right hand of my righteousness. Isaiah 41:10

But they that wait upon the Lord shall renew their strength; they shall mount up with wings as eagles; they shall run, and not be weary; and they shall walk, and not faint. Isaiah 40:31

And let us not grow weary of doing good, for in due season we will reap, if we do not give up. Galatians 6:9

Trust in the Lord with all thine heart; and lean not unto thine own understanding. In all thy ways acknowledge him, and he shall direct thy paths. Proverbs 3:5-6

Clean Slate

Just like the ocean waves on that distant beach, they continue to keep rolling in;
They are your dreams, memories, hopes, desires, regrets and the occasional sin.

That's what our lives are truly made of when all is said and done;
All mixed together and tumbling to and fro together with each new rising sun.

Some people just play it safe and never have any regrets until it's too late it seems;
But when they look back on their lives, how many discover so many unfulfilled dreams.

Others take it to the extreme and live life full of regrets and sin each day;
Then they wonder just how they ever went so far astray.

It's never too late to new start over and make a new beginning they say;
You just need to let go and let God and start fresh with each new day.

Put the past behind you and look to a future so bright, clean and clear;
This is your new life and a fresh clean slate so go forward with God and have no fear.

Live your life to the fullest each day, always doing and giving the best that you can;
Then when you reach the end of life's trail, you'll know that you really did give it all and had a plan.

So saddle up and ride into this new future that awaits you down this dusty road;
This is your life and your choices to make so live life each day to its fullest and ride into the future, now go boldly go.

∾∾∾

For I know the thoughts that I think toward you, saith the Lord, thoughts of peace, and not of evil, to give you an expected end. Jeremiah 29:11

For God hath not given us the spirit of fear; but of power, and of love, and of a sound mind. 2 Timothy 1:7

And we know that all things work together for good to them that love God, to them who are the called according to his purpose. Romans 8:28

Be sober, be vigilant; because your adversary the devil, as a roaring lion, walks about, seeking whom he may devour: 1 Peter 5:8

Delight thyself also in the Lord: and he shall give thee the desires of thine heart. Psalm 37:4

All we like sheep have gone astray; we have turned everyone to his own way; and the Lord hath laid on him the iniquity of us all. Isaiah 53:6

Trust in the Lord with all thine heart; and lean not unto thine own understanding. In all thy ways acknowledge him, and he shall direct thy paths. Proverbs 3:5-6

Wherefore we labor, that, whether present or absent, we may be accepted of him. For we must all appear before the judgment seat of Christ; that every one may receive the things done in his body, according to that he hath done, whether it be good or bad. 2 Corinthians 5:9-10

Therefore if any man be in Christ, he is a new creature: old things are passed away; behold all things are become new. 2 Corinthians 5:17

It's Never Easy

The windows were wide open and the curtains bristled in the breeze;
This was her first fall in Colorado and she wondered about the earliest freeze.

It was for her a new beginning, and that meant for her a brand new start;
Golden was the place she had found to create a new life and to mend her broken heart.

Sometimes life doesn't go the way you had it all planned, it seems;
You just have to cowgirl up and occasionally bury those wrecked dreams.

It's never easy to start over this she knew way down deep inside;
But her faith was strong and she knew that God would somehow provide.

The view of the sun glistening off the Rockies always took her breath away;
It was in the quiet of the early morning that she always took time to pray.

She remembered reading a poem one day of how much better it could all be;
Reading how it was really up to her now and to pray, perceive and then really believe and make ready to receive.

Change and new beginnings don't really seem to happen all that fast;
Then one day she met the cowboy of her dreams and knew this was destined to last.

Weeks and months went by and the closer to each other they both grew;
One night on bended knee he asked for her hand then next they both said, "I do".

Now they ride together through the meadows with the majestic Rockies hovering high above;
Side by side they ride feeling so blessed and so very much in love.

So never give up on love or the dreams you carry deep within;
Always keep trusting in God as he'll never take you where He
hasn't already been.

∼∼∼

*Behold, I will do a new thing; now it shall spring forth; shall ye not know
it? I will even make a way in the wilderness, and rivers in the desert.
Isaiah 43:19*

*Therefore if any man be in Christ, he is a new creature: old things are
passed away; behold all things are become new.
2 Corinthians 5:17*

*The Lord is near to the brokenhearted and saves the crushed in spirit.
Psalm 34:18*

*Finally, brethren, whatsoever things are true, whatsoever things are
honest, whatsoever things are just, whatsoever things are pure,
whatsoever things are lovely, whatsoever things are of good report; if
there be any virtue, and if there be any praise, think on these things.
Philippians 4:8*

*Therefore I say unto you, What things so ever ye desire, when ye pray,
believe that ye receive them, and ye shall have them.
Mark 11:24*

*d in the morning, rising up a great while before day, he went out, and
departed into a solitary place, and there prayed. Mark 1:35*

*Nevertheless let every one of you in particular so love his wife even as
himself; and the wife see that she reverence her husband. Ephesians
5:33*

*And let us not grow weary of doing good, for in due season we will reap,
if we do not give up. Galatians 6:9*

*Now the God of hope fill you with all joy and peace in believing, that ye
may abound in hope, through the power of the Holy Ghost. Romans
15:13*

*And they that know thy name will put their trust in thee: for thou, LORD,
hast not forsaken them that seek thee. Psalm 9:10*

*Delight thyself also in the LORD: and he shall give thee the desires of
thine heart Psalm 37:4*

Texas Dance Hall

There he came as she watched him purposely stride through the Gruene Hall door;
Not another dime store cowboy she thought, but the real deal and so very much more.

He went to one of the bars, tipped his black Stetson and ordered himself a drink;
The way that lady bartender smiled he must have said something to make her really think.

Turning his back to the bar he seemed to watch everyone just taking it all in;
Next, their eyes both locked on one another together feeling it deep down within.

Slowly he tipped his hat in her direction and she smiled a big smile back at him;
Then leisurely he strolled over to her and asked her if she'd dance with him seemingly on a whim.

As he took her hand he escorted her over to the dance floor beyond;
Holding her close they danced and twirled the night away and both started feeling a close bond.

Oh my, she thought as they two-stepped and he twirled her around and around dance after dance;
Was this as she had once dreamed the beginning of a real cowboy and cowgirl romance?

Now down life's trail, they travel through life together side by side and hand n hand;
It all came together in a Texas dance hall while listening to a red dirt band.

~~~

A time to weep, and a time to laugh; a time to mourn, and a time to dance; Ecclesiastes 3:4

Let them praise his name in the dance: let them sing praises unto him with the timbrel and harp. Psalm 149:3

Let your fountain be blessed, and rejoice in the wife of your youth, a lovely deer, a graceful doe. Let her breasts fill you at all times with delight; be intoxicated always in her love. Proverbs 5:18-19

Then the Lord God said, "It is not good that the man should be alone; I will make him a helper fit for him." Genesis 2:18

I am my beloved's and my beloved is mine; Song of Solomon 6:3

And above all these put on love, which binds everything together in perfect harmony. Colossians 3:14

As a lily among brambles, so is my love among the young women. Song of Solomon 2:2

So they are no longer two but one flesh. What therefore God has joined together, let not man separate." Matthew 19:6

So we have come to know and to believe the love that God has for us. God is love, and whoever abides in love abides in God, and God abides in him. 1 John 4:16

So now faith, hope, and love abide, these three; but the greatest of these is love. 1 Corinthians 13:13

Above all, keep loving one another earnestly, since love covers a multitude of sins. 1 Peter 4:8

Hopes and Dreams

The darkness and coolness of the night seemed to come on so fast and envelope him like a black veil;
In the distance, he could hear the loneliness of a lone coyotes wail.

Many miles he had ridden down this lonely trail for countless days it seems;
So many more miles yet to go, then he and she could begin again living their lifelong dream.

Wars dark side had left him wounded, hardened and older before his time;
His only prayer was that she was safe and still loved him like in that ole cowboy's rhyme.

A few more days down this long Texas trail and he knew that shed again be in his arms;
Then once again he'd taste the sweetness of her kisses and feel her loving charms.

She grabbed the Winchester when saw a lone cowboy high up on the ridge just after noon;
How many times she felt the fear when a stranger appeared and hoped he'd be back soon.

With her hand to her brow, she noticed the way he sat the saddle and realized it was him;
Thanking God that now with war's end they could really begin again.

As he galloped down the hill on his horse, she ran to him flat out followed by their hound;
He dismounted at full speed and they collapsed in each other's arms onto the freshly plowed ground.

They embraced so tightly and kissed so long as their passion seemed to fill the air;
Now they were together again and free from fear and without care.

It was for them a chance for a new beginning in this place they both dearly loved to be;
To build a future on those dreams they once had and now make them all a reality.

So never give up on your hopes and dreams no matter how hard the trail has been to ride;
Trust in God above and let your love for each other continue to grow as you put your fears aside.

∽∽∽

And God shall wipe away all tears from their eyes; and there shall be no more death, neither sorrow, nor crying, neither shall there be any more pain: for the former things are passed away. Revelation 21:4

Let him kiss me with the kisses of his mouth: for thy love is better than wine. Song of Solomon 1:2

What therefore God hath joined together, let not man put asunder. Mark 10:9

Giving thanks always for all things unto God and the Father in the name of our Lord Jesus Christ; Ephesians 5:20

Husbands, love your wives, even as Christ also loved the church, and gave himself for it; Ephesians 5:25

And now these three remain: faith, hope and love. But the greatest of these is love. 1 Corinthians 13:13

Fear thou not; for I am with thee: be not dismayed; for I am thy God: I will strengthen thee; yea, I will help thee; yea, I will uphold thee with the right hand of my righteousness. Isaiah 41:10

And let us not grow weary of doing good, for in due season we will reap, if we do not give up. Galatians 6:9

Trust in the Lord with all thine heart; and lean not unto thine own understanding. In all thy ways acknowledge him, and he shall direct thy paths. Proverbs 3:5-6

And this I pray, that your love may abound yet more and more in knowledge and in all judgment; Philippians 1:9

Delight thyself also in the Lord: and he shall give thee the desires of thine heart. Commit thy way unto the Lord; trust also in him; and he shall bring it to pass. Psalm 37:4-5

Win Lose or Draw

He tightened his cinch and made sure his rope and saddle were just right;
They had come to Vegas as a roping team hoping to make some real money tonight.

The calf was on its run and he broke the barrier right on the line;
He got the head aligned and his partner got the heels in record time.

Rodeo can be a great metaphor for everyday life it sometimes seems;
You're never really are all alone when you come together and work in concert as a team.

Sometimes in rodeo just like it is in real life things can go off course making you want to scream;
You miss a loop or stumble and all seems lost along with your gold buckle dreams.

You just have to cowboy up each time and never think of ever giving in;
This could be the time you and your partner finally the gold buckle do win.

So it is with our Heavenly Father as He watches the rodeo from up on high above;
He's always riding with and watching over you with His mercy and forgiving love.

So never give up on life or your main team member, keep trusting in God as he rides with you by your side;
Just keep trusting God and win lose or draw, always thank Him for another ride.

~~~

Not many of you should become teachers, my brothers, for you know that we who teach will be judged with greater strictness. James 3:1

I can do all things through Christ which strengthened me. Philippians 4:13

But thanks be to God, which giveth us the victory through our Lord Jesus Christ. 1 Corinthians 15:57

And every man that striveth for the mastery is temperate in all things. Now they do it to obtain a corruptible crown; but we an incorruptible. 1 Corinthians 9:25

Two are better than one; because they have a good reward for their labour. Ecclesiastes 4:9

For God hath not given us the spirit of fear; but of power, and of love, and of a sound mind. 2 Timothy 1:7 ESV

I can do all things through Christ which strengthened me. Philippians 4:13

Seek the Lord and his strength, seek his face continually. 1 Chronicles 16:11

And let us not grow weary of doing good, for in due season we will reap, if we do not give up. Galatians 6:9

Delight thyself also in the Lord: and he shall give thee the desires of thine heart. Commit thy way unto the Lord; trust also in him; and he shall bring it to pass. Psalm 37:4-5

Christmas Dream

They had met at a Texas dance hall when she walked up and asked him to dance;
He told her that he wasn't that good but if she was willing, let's take a chance.

She whispered to him that he'd underestimated his dance skills and did he always come here on Fridays?
Then the band played a waltz and she was even more amazed as he whirled her around leaving her in a daze.

Spending the rest of the evening just dancing and talking the night away;
Each time he held her close dancing she felt as if she was in some romantic ballet.

He told her he was new to San Antonio and that this was his first time here tonight;
Have you been to the River Walk she asked, it's really beautiful this time of year with all the lights.

No, he replied, would you consider being my guide and showing me the town?
So they made a date for the next Friday night for her to show him around.

Later he walked her out to her Mercedes ragtop and twirled her around kissing her on her lips;
Oh my, she thought feeling electricity going from her lips to her fingertips.

Talking over the week the closer they became as she was beginning to feel blessed;
Maybe she thought there was a real cowboy at last that would pass loves test.

Such an amazing sight where all the Christmas lights all along the River Walk;
Walking hand 'n hand to a little restaurant where they could sit and talk.

Let's leave your truck at my condo parking garage and let me take you out to my ranch when we leave;

Think it would be better if I drive as I wouldn't want to lose you in the breeze.

Along winding country roads they drove out deep into the countryside;
Driving she pointed out points of interest trying her best to be a good tour guide.

Pulling up to a large double wide gate with a Texas brand right there front and center;
Here he was sitting, next to a beautiful Texas Angel feeling like earthly heaven he was about to enter.

Down the road a piece was a great Christmas tree decorated from bottom to top with lights;
Seeing a house on the left he commented nice, smiling she said that's the guest house but not for you tonight.

Upon another hill there he saw it majestically standing decorated like it was a downtown hotel;
Cowboy thought he'd seen it all, but his friends would never believe this if he ever decided to tell.

The Cowboy and the Lady came together at Midnight Rodeo and each other did redeem;
Smiling they remember back to that special Christmas when for each was fulfilled a Christmas dream.

∾∾∾

Delight yourself in the Lord, and he will give you the desires of your heart. Psalm 37:4

For still the vision awaits its appointed time; it hastens to the end—it will not lie. If it seems slow, wait for it; it will surely come; it will not delay. Habakkuk 2:3

Trust in the Lord with all your heart, and do not lean on your own understanding. In all your ways acknowledge him, and he will make straight your paths. Proverbs 3:5-6

And let us not grow weary of doing good, for in due season we will reap, if we do not give up. Galatians 6:9

Whoso finds a wife found a good thing, and obtained favor of the Lord. Proverbs 18:22

So now faith, hope, and love abide, these three; but the greatest of these is love. 1 Corinthians 13:13

The Broken Spoke

What a vision was she that just seemed to have walked out of some cowboys dream;
She had long flowing dark hair and deep blue eyes in a pair of Wranglers that fit every seam.

Wasn't here to hear some cowboy's latest tale or some old line;
Or to be some cowboy's next conquest by being told, she was so fine.

It's all been said in other times and places and she's heard most of it long before;
It was going to take more than some cowboy Casanova to get her onto that dance floor.

This was her first time back at The Broken Spoke, a legendary dance hall in Austin town;
But this night she was just here for the music and not to be fooled and danced around.

Once she was the singer in the band and up on that very stage singing her songs;
That was in her past but on the stage is where she always felt that she belongs.

Then there he stood at the edge of her table as she slowly raised her eyes;
Black Stetson over piercing brown eyes as her memory replayed her real surprise.

Almost jumping to her feet she gave that cowboy a big ole hug and kiss;
Memories came flooding back to both of them to another time and romantic bliss.

You never know where true love will find you even if you're down and blue;
Just keep believing and maybe some ole flame will walk back into your life and make it feel brand new.

~~~

*You are altogether beautiful, my love; there is no flaw in you.
Song of Solomon 4:7*

*Behold, you are beautiful, my love, behold, you are beautiful!
Song of Solomon 4:1*

Blessed is she who has believed that the Lord would fulfill his promises to her!"Luke 1:45

She is more precious than jewels, and nothing you desire can compare with her. Proverbs 3:15

*Singers and dancers alike say, "All my springs are in you."
Psalm 87:7*

So now faith, hope, and love abide, these three; but the greatest of these is love.1 Corinthians 13:13

And above all these put on love, which binds everything together in perfect harmony. Colossians 3:14

With all humility and gentleness, with patience, bearing with one another in love, Ephesians 4:2

Let him kiss me with the kisses of his mouth! For your love is better than wine; Song of Solomon 1:2

Take delight in the Lord, and he will give you the desires of your heart. Psalm 37:4

*For where your treasure is, there your heart will be also.
Matthew 6:21*

The Real Deal

Like most people in life she had that one special dream that she carried deep inside;
To find that one special cowboy man and go riding through life side by side.

Could this cowboy be the one that was sent and came dancing into her life;
Is he the one God chose to send to her so maybe she one day would become his wife.

At first, she hadn't given it much thought after having been burned in the past;
Was he for real, the one rhymes talked about with a true love that would last?

Days turned into weeks then months just seemed to go flying by;
Closer and closer they became and one day she just stopped wondering if or why?

He got her attention on their first date when he took her hand and said grace before they did eat;
Then the time they were camping and he warmed up some water to wash her muddy feet.

There was that awkward conversation that they had early on the phone;
When they talked about what real love and marriage were and what it meant before Gods throne.

Many times she wondered and thought if this cowboy was really for real;
Then as time went on she realized and was sure that he was, in fact, the real deal.

So never doubt or give up on Gods plans to direct you to the perfect love;
He's always with you trying to lead and guide your steps from up above.

∾∾∾

Delight thyself also in the Lord: and he shall give thee the desires of thine heart. Psalm 37:4

Whoso findeth a wife findeth a good thing, and obtaineth favour of the Lord. Proverbs 18:22

Love is patient and kind; love does not envy or boast; it is not arrogant or rude. It does not insist on its own way; it is not irritable or resentful; it does not rejoice at wrongdoing, but rejoices with the truth. 1 Corinthians 13:4-6

And we know that all things work together for good to them that love God, to them who are the called according to his purpose. Romans 8:28

Remember ye not the former things, neither consider the things of old. Isaiah 43:18

And when he had thus spoken, he took bread, and gave thanks to God in presence of them all: and when he had broken it, he began to eat. Acts 27:35

Fear thou not; for I am with thee: be not dismayed; for I am thy God: I will strengthen thee; yea, I will help thee; yea, I will uphold thee with the right hand of my righteousness. Isaiah 41:10

Then turning toward the woman he said to Simon, "Do you see this woman? I entered your house; you gave me no water for my feet, but she has wet my feet with her tears and wiped them with her hair. Luke 7:44

And let us not grow weary of doing good, for in due season we will reap, if we do not give up. Galatians 6:9

I will instruct thee and teach thee in the way which thou shalt go: I will guide thee with mine eye. Psalm 32:8

More books by Michael Gasaway

Desires of Your Heart

Angels and Cowboys

Life's Highway and Dusty Trails

Available on Amazon

Or At

www.MichaelGasaway.com

And on Facebook at

https://www.facebook.com/michaelthepoetryman

Coming later this year or early next year a novel of true love, desire and passion:

Once Upon a Lifetime

Made in the USA
Columbia, SC
21 May 2019